The Sailing Ship Tree

The Sailing Ship Tree
A Liverpool Story

Berlie Doherty

Catnip

CATNIP BOOKS
Published by Catnip Publishing Ltd.
14 Greville Street
London EC1N 8SB

This edition published 2008
Copyright © 1998 Berlie Doherty

1 3 5 7 9 10 8 6 4 2

A CIP catalogue record for this book is available from the British Library

ISBN 978-1-84647-044-8

Printed in Poland EU, produced by Polskabook

www.catnippublishing.co.uk

To my brother and sister, Denis and Jean, in memory of Dad.

My father, Walter Hollingsworth, loved to write stories and gave me a lot of encouragement. This book is a collaboration between us, as it is inspired by some of the stories about his childhood that I found after he died, aged ninety-three.

The members of the Hollins family are based on Arthur, Mary Jane, Harold, Dorothy and Walter Hollingsworth. All the other characters are fictitious, though the big house, Bark Hill, was a real place.

Contents

Dorothy

The Sailing Ship Tree

*W*e lived with the sound of the trees. We could hear them day and night, sighing and whispering as if they had great secrets to tell. When the wind turned with the changing tide they would sing a different song. And then, one day, they stopped their singing and we knew we would never hear them again.

We are Dorothy and Walter. Dorothy Alice and Walter Alfred William Hollins. We're twins. We've never played together much. But we think together, that's the main thing. We know what's going on, almost without telling each other. And this story belongs to both of us, but it's a long time since it all happened. We're old, old people now. But we don't forget the trees, the wonderful swaying trees, and the day the trees stopped singing.

We're not the only children in the story. There's Mary, the tweeny. And there's Master George. It's mostly about him. And about the Big House. In a way, the Big House belong to all of us.

From our bedroom we could see the crashing heads of the great sycamores on the drive. When they were in full leaf they sounded like the waves on the Dingle shore. In autumn the leaves fluttered like golden banners, and in winter they floated down on their papery wings and had to be uprooted from our garden. We always used to look out at them, first thing, as soon as Ma called us to come down for our breakfast.

There was a chestnut tree too, and that was our favourite. It looked like a great sailing ship. Sometimes there would be a message for us hidden in a secret hole in one of its branches. But that comes much later in the story.

Let's start, oh, on 7 May 1910. We were nearly nine years old then. All that time ago. We can both remember that day very well, even though we were so young at the time.

No Place for Twins Here

Harry was snoring, his nose stuck inside the pillow of feathers like a fox in a shed of hens. There was only one bedroom in the cottage, and all five of us slept in it. There were two beds: a big iron one for Ma and Pa, with brass knobs on the rail that could be twisted right off; a squeaky one for us; and Harry slept on a lumpy horsehair mattress on the floor. There was a piece of sprigged muslin on a string acting as a curtain between the mattress and our bed, and Walter spent most of his time squirming under it to borrow Harry's comics. Ma said she was going to swap us round soon, so I would have the mattress and Walter and Harry would share the bed. I couldn't imagine it.

Walter and I climbed over the big bed that Ma and Pa used and chased each other downstairs. Ma had some water ready in the jug for us to wash ourselves, and we sat by the stove and ate the porridge she'd made. Nat, the under-gardener's son, had brought us a comb of golden, sticky honey the day before, and we swirled a trickle of it over our porridge. Walter licked the spoon, curling his tongue round and round it.

'Harry won't get any,' Ma said, her mouth in a tight little line, 'because he won't get up.'

But when he did come down, scratching and yawning and smelling of sleep, she gave him his share. As soon as he'd eaten, he was off to work on his bike, with a hunk of bread and cheese in one pocket and a bottle of tea in the other. He was nearly fourteen and had just got a job as an errand boy for a shipping firm out on the docks. He behaved like a grown-up now, full of himself. Too big for his boots, Ma said.

'Can I run down with you?' Walter asked him. 'I won't be late for school.'

'No, you can't,' Ma said quickly. 'You're too young, it's too far, and it's windy . . . just look at that wind in the trees – it'd blow you right over the Mersey. And besides, I've got a job for you two.'

We looked at each other and pulled faces. Ma rarely gave us separate jobs to do. It was as if we were one person and everything had to be shared between us. Why, when we were very little we were even dressed the same, with frocks and with ribbons in our long yellow curls. Then came the day the photographer was sent down from the Big House, and Walter was put in a blue sailor suit and had his hair cut short. For our fifth birthday, that was. I'll never forget that day. I couldn't stop staring at him. It was as if I'd been cut in half. All of a sudden Walter didn't look like me, he looked like himself. Can you imagine that? Ma didn't say anything about it, but she picked up one of the locks of his hair and put it upstairs in the chest.

'I want you to go up the Big House,' Ma said, not that

day but the day we're talking about, 'and enquire after His Majesty.'

Walter gaped at me with his porridge dripping off his spoon. The only time we were ever allowed to go right up to the Big House was at Christmas, when we were invited to a party with all the other servants and their families and given presents by Miss Caroline. We weren't even allowed to walk on the drive where the carriages went, though Walter and Harry often climbed up the trees and hid there, safe in the cover of flickering leaves, still as stick insects, spying on the gentry.

If we were actually in the grounds or at church and saw any of the gentry I had to bob a curtsey and Walter had to take off his cap. Miss Caroline would smile at us but Miss Victoria would stare right through us as if she could see out the other side.

'Are we to go to the big door?' Walter asked. I knew he was thinking of the great brass bell that hung there and I was wondering if we would be tall enough to reach the rope that made it clang.

Ma's mouth set in its tight little line again. 'Not even today,' she said. 'Go and find Pa, and if you can't find him, ask the cook. But be respectful, mind,' she called after us. 'And don't dilly-dally. You've to get to school on time, even today.'

It was always Walter who went first. He had been born first, after all, and, anyway, he could run faster. But he had a stammer that used to trip him up when he was least expecting it, especially when he was speaking to adults, and when he got tongue-tied it would be me who had to do the talking. I always knew what he wanted to say.

He darted towards the kitchen gardens and the servants' territory at the back of the house, and I stumbled after him. He was a nuisance, running so fast. He knew it annoyed me, too. And I was a bit afraid once we were out of the cover of the rhododendron bushes, because at any moment Mawks, the head gardener, might appear ducking and grumbling out of one of the greenhouses and bellow at us to get back home.

I was relieved to see Nat. He waved at us cheerfully and carried on raking the soil between the rows of cabbages. Jackdaws hopped about around his legs, and every so often he would wave his arms and shoo them away. Their cries rang out like pistol shots. 'Jack! Jack!'

'I don't want to go any further,' I panted, as we rounded the last greenhouse and reached the cobbled yard by the stables.

'Hang about here then,' said Walter, impatient to get our errand done. 'All the gentry are upstairs anyway. There's no danger.'

'Yes there is. There's Bains.'

That was true. There was Bains, the housekeeper, with her jangly keys and her starched white face, and her boots that snapped when she walked. She was over all the servants except Pa, and Ma said she'd sent many a serving girl crying back to her family, because they weren't up to standard. We both stopped and wondered if we dared try to get past her. What if she was the one who answered the door?

'We won't knock at the door,' Walter decided.

'Will we just run in?'

'She's no more important than Pa.'

'And there's the rocking horse.'

'Pooh,' said Walter. 'There's no rocking horse. That's just a story.'

Well, it was a story that all the servants in the Big House told us though, so it must have been true. Down in the cellars there was a rocking horse that rocked all by itself. It didn't bear thinking about.

'Don't make me go in, Walter.'

I edged towards one of the outhouses as Walter ran up to the kitchen door. The kitchen maid was hauling on the squeaking pump in the yard. She was younger than Harry and looked thin and gawky in a black dress that was too long and loose for her and a white cap that nearly covered her eyes. A hiss of water swished into the bucket. She walked across the yard carefully carrying the water bucket by one hand and a bucket of scraps for Miss Victoria's cats by the other. She was too intent on not spilling them to take any notice of us.

'H-Hello,' Walter said, and without looking up, she blew a wisp of hair from her face and said, 'Good morning, twins.'

Walter slipped through the black hole of the servants' door. A horse stamped in the stable behind me and at the last minute I made a dash for it and followed Walter in. I dodged after him along the damp passage. I knew one of the doors led down to the cellar where the rocking horse was kept, and I held my breath and ran. In the kitchen Joan, the cook, glanced up and saw us running in. She was carrying a steaming pan and her face was red and gleaming with sweat.

'No place for twins here,' she muttered, and tipped the water with a scalding whoosh into a bowl. One of the maids looked up from her chopping and jerked her head towards the butler's pantry, and Walter went proudly forward and tapped on the door. Two game birds hung from a beam above his head, and there were maggots crawling over them like rolling pearly beads. We waited, breathless, for the grunt Pa would make in answer to Walter's knock, and then crept inside.

'Hello, Pa,' Walter said, in a quiet little voice as if he was in church.

Pa stood with his back to us, a green baize apron tied around his waist and the starched cuffs of his shirt pushed above his powdery elbows. He still had his white gloves on though. He was intent on his task of counting out pieces of silver cutlery to put in the big cupboard. There was a big fire blazing in his fireplace and a comfy-looking red chair at the side of it. It was bigger than the room in the cottage where we all had to live and eat. Next to the window, a bright-yellow canary bobbed and trilled in its cage. I never knew till then that Pa had a canary.

Pa continued to count under his breath until he had all the knives and forks and spoons nestled away in their own felt compartments. Then he closed the door with its big brass knob and locked it. He turned gravely, rolling his sleeves back down with quick jerks of his wrists. 'Now, Walter.'

'Ma sent us to ask you what news there is of the King. Please, Pa.'

Pa untied his apron and hung it on a hook beside the door, moving Walter to one side so he could reach it. He lifted down his long-tailed jacket and put it back on. He hated to be seen without it, even in front of us.

'The king is dead,' he said, bowing his head so his voice was deep and grave in his throat. 'He died last night. Now run home, twins. You shouldn't be here, you know that. Yes – ' He tinkled his fingernail along the ribs of the canary cage – 'His Majesty is no more.'

We ran back out through the kitchen and along the passage into the blue day. We were quiet and thrilled and shocked, and my heart was big in my chest with the grown-up news. Edward the Seventh, the king of England and the Empire, was dead.

'What happens now?' I said. 'How can we manage without a king?'

Ma nodded grimly when we reported the news.

'Well, it's over then. I thought as much. Now dash off to school,' she told us. 'And tell Miss Brogan. She may not know yet.'

'But what happens when the king dies?' I asked. I imagined England sailing like a ship without a captain into the fog of the Mersey, never to be seen again; a ghost ship, with sad voices crying out from it in the still of the night.

'Oh, the country will get another king, and that will be George.'

'Master George!' I gasped, and Ma laughed, which was a rare thing.

'Bless you, no! He's only a gentleman's son! A different George, the son of Edward. And Heaven help us if he's as bad as his father.'

'I wish it would be Master George,' said Walter. 'Then he'd ask me to be his butler. The young king, and Walter Hollins, the youngest butler in the world . . .'

'Gentleman's gentleman,' Ma corrected him, swabbing at my hair with a brush as I tried to wriggle away. Walter wasn't listening. He was going to write a story about this, I could tell.

'. . . And the best,' he went on, 'and every night, after the king had finished talking to his prime minister, he and Walter Hollins would climb the tallest tree in the palace garden and survey the kingdom.'

'Never mind the kingdom, what about school!' Ma said. She whacked my bottom gently with the back of the brush. 'You'll have to run like billy-o!'

I grabbed my skipping rope for playtime and pushed it into my pinafore pocket. Walter was streaking ahead, and he was out in the road before I'd reached the servants' gate. I saw him waving to a cart driver.

'I have a message to deliver to the king!' he called. 'I cannot delay!'

There was a shout and the sound of rumbling wheels. A brown carthorse trotted up and nuzzled his wet lips against my neck, making me giggle and squirm. His appley breath steamed round my face. Salty jerked the reins to pull Elijah's long head away from me, snorting just like his horse.

'Late again, twins!' Salty said in his gritty voice. We loved Salty. His nose was pocked like a strawberry, and his eyes were rheumy and blue. He was the nicest old person we knew, because he didn't seem to mind that we were only children, and he talked to us about anything and anybody. When he came to our cottage he always stopped for a mug of tea, which he would drink still sitting in his cart, while Elijah cropped our grass and rolled mournful eyes at Ma, hoping for sugar lumps.

'The king's dead,' I told him, proud to be first with the news.

Salty pushed his old cap to one side and scratched his head. White grains of salt shivered out of his hair. 'Is he now? It's come at last. What's to do now then?' He puffed out his lips and stared into the space between Elijah's ears, as if there was an answer there.

'Are you going past the school?' I asked, knowing he wasn't really, and a bit embarrassed by his silence. I wondered if he might be going to cry.

'He liked the company of beautiful women,' Salty said, as if he was reciting the king's epitaph. 'Well, come on.' He started up, his old self again, and jerked Elijah's reins. 'Climb aboard!'

The floor of his cart was white and powdery and we had to lean back against his big block of salt, listening to his grumblings about the number of people who owed him money. We knew who all the bad payers on the Estate were, and I'm pleased to say Ma wasn't one of them.

He took us straight on to school and left us by the gates. We could hear the shouting of the other children, the lashing of whips across tops and the beat of ropes on the earth, and the steady chanting of the girls as they skipped. *'The big ship sails on the illy-allyo, the illy-allyo, the illy-allyo . . .'* There was a gate for boys and a gate for girls, and we both ran in, forgetting each other for the moment.

Our teacher was Miss Brogan, tall as a flagpole and just as thin, with huge brown shiny wet eyes. She was already in the yard, and as she rang her bell we all ran into our lines and followed her silently into the classroom.

'Wish I was Master George,' Walter whispered. 'He never goes to school.'

Miss Brogan frowned at him, flaring her nostrils out, reminding me just for a minute of old Elijah.

'Miss Brogan.' I approached her timidly. 'Ma said I was to tell you that the king is dead.'

Miss Brogan was flustered, her Saturday-morning routine broken. 'We will go home,' she said. 'Wait! We will first pray for His Majesty's soul. Put your hands together, children. May he rest in peace.'

'Amen, Miss Brogan.' We stood with our heads bowed, solemn and a little afraid now. When I looked up quickly I saw that Hannah Patterson in front of me had a dirty neck underneath her yellow ringlets.

'Go quietly,' Miss Brogan said, 'and on Monday come in your clothes of mourning. The whole country will be showing its respects to His Majesty.'

But the sky outside was the colour of the bluebells in our woods, and we didn't want to walk quietly. The seagulls over our heads were coasting like white ships on the ocean, and we wanted to open out our arms like wings and circle and soar with them, and scream out loud.

That night, Pa woke us up from our sleep, and asked us to come downstairs. There was no rousing Harry, so we climbed over his body and crept down the stairs, mystified, hauling our blanket between us to wrap over our shoulders. It was midnight, but the sky was only just dark. The stars were coming through bright and fierce, and there was one that was bigger than the rest, and a queer shape, with a light like a horse's tail trailing behind it.

'That's Halley's comet,' Pa said, crouching down to us. He was whispering. 'That trail like a lady's hair is ice dust. It will never come again in my lifetime. Not for another seventy-five years. You've seen a wonderful thing tonight. A very special thing. Never forget it.'

'No, Pa,' we both whispered back, as if we were still in the classroom saying Amen.

'That's enough now,' Ma called softly from the doorway. 'Bring them back in.' But she didn't send us off to bed. She gave us hot milk and we sat by the last of the fire warming our hands round the mugs.

'We'll be eighty-four,' said Walter, who had taken all

that time to work it out. Ma laughed and pulled us to her, and her breath was warm and milky.

'Miss Brogan said we have to wear our mourning clothes for school,' I said. 'I don't like them, Ma.'

'At least they should still fit you. It seems no time at all since we were wearing mourning for the poor Mistress, God rest her soul.'

The quiet time was over. We were pushed upstairs to our bed, and Ma rummaged through the trunk and brought out the black funeral clothes that we had worn the year before, when Master George's mother had died.

If You Know Your Place

W*e* haven't told you about Master George yet, not really. He lived in the Big House where Pa worked as the butler and where Ma used to work as a lady's maid to the Mistress until she and Pa got married. The Mistress used to take rides round the Estate sometimes in her pony and trap. That was the only time we ever saw Master George. He was with his mother or his nanny all the time, and they never let him out of their sight. He used to stare at us as if he longed to jump out of the trap and run and play with us, but Ma said the family was very strict with him; too strict. He sometimes played with his cousins when they came to stay. But when his mother died it was as if the Big House had swallowed him up, and we only ever saw him at church after that.

His father was one of the rich men of Liverpool, or at least he acted like it. We found out later that all his money belonged to the Dowager, but her brains had gone soft and she didn't know what to do with it anyway. She used to be a society beauty, Ma said. I couldn't imagine it at all. We hardly ever saw her, only when she was being pushed around by Timothy, the footman, in her Bath chair. We saw even less of the master, Mister Leighton.

He was something to do with ships and he was always going away somewhere.

You should have seen the fuss when he came back home! The Old Dowager always insisted on holding a party for him. Ma said it was because she loved to watch the music and the dancing so much. It reminded her of when she was the belle of the ball. Imagine! All the gardeners would be busy for days beforehand, getting up vegetables and flowers for the House, and supplies of meat and fish would be brought in from town. And then the gentry's carriages would come sweeping up the long drive, with their proud horses prancing and their brasses gleaming. It was a grand sight to see, and we never missed it. The boys would be up a tree and I would be under a rhododendron bush.

So then there was Miss Victoria, who didn't care for parties at all. Later we found out she was wicked. And there was little Miss Caroline, dreamy-eyed like a happy cat. We loved her. She used to send a catalogue down just before Christmas so we could choose our presents. We were given them at the servants' party, and all the gentry would come down and smile at us, except for Miss Victoria, who didn't know what a smile was. And the Dowager would be wheeled round in her Bath chair and would reach out and squeeze your hand, and hers felt as papery as dry leaves.

'I'm frightened of the old one,' I said on the way home from one of these Christmas 'do's. All the other servants had been there, even the farm labourers who worked the fields, stiff and awkward in their best clothes. As soon as they got outside they were loosening their collars as if they were trying to breathe again, like Mawks' dog trying to get off his lead. Walter had been given a football and I had been given a whip and a wooden spinning top painted green. I was cracking my whip as I went, making the frost on the grass shower up.

'You! You've no need to be frightened of her!' Ma said. 'You've no need to have anything to do with her. Just keep away if you know your place.'

'But what is my place?'

'Servant. If we know our place, and the gentry know theirs, there's no reason why we shouldn't get along very well.'

'I feel sorry for Master George, having Miss Victoria for a sister,' said Walter.

'Oh, don't you worry your head about Master George! He's got plenty of money to make up for it,' Ma laughed. She was very merry that day. It wasn't often she would talk about the gentry like this.

'But does it make up for it?' I asked.

And Ma looked down at me in that quiet way she sometimes had, a way of cupping her hand under her chin as if it made her think better.

'No, sweetheart. No. I don't suppose it does,' she said.

'Poor Master George then.'

The Finest Ship in the World

The young master, that's what they call me. I live at the top of our house, Bark Hill. I hardly ever see my sisters, Victoria and Caroline, apart from having lunch every day with them. I hardly ever see anybody since Mama died and Nanny was sent away. When Mama was alive I used to go out every day with her, and if we saw the servants' children they would bob to us and run away like rabbits. 'Can I play with them?' I used to ask. 'No, George. You're a gentleman's son. Remember that.'

I have to get up at six o'clock every day for lessons. At first I had a governess. She was German and she spent most of her days weeping for home because she missed the mountains so much. It was rather embarrassing. But while she was sitting at the table with her face buried in a handkerchief and I was pretending not to notice, I could look over her shoulder and see right down across the lawns. I watched the horses pulling the hay wagons across the fields, and the children of the farm workers running about like frisky colts. How I wished I could be allowed to play with them. Beyond them, I could see the River Mersey leading out to the Bay of Liverpool. I could see the sailing ships coming in and out like huge swans floating on the river, and the tugboats, and the great steamers. It makes me proud to see these, because some of them belong to my father. When I grow up they will belong to me.

One day the weeping governess just gave up and went home to her mountains, without a word of farewell to anyone, and I had a whole winter without lessons. But I still had to stay in the schoolroom because there was nowhere else for me to go, unless I sidled down the servants' stairs and begged Cook for a bit of cake, or into my Grandmother the Dowager's room to read to her. Then I was allowed to choose books from the library next to Victoria's drawing room. My favourite tale was *Pirate* by Sir Walter Scott, but Victoria has forbidden me to read anything so lively. The Dowager kept it hidden for me in her doll's house. But reading to her was a chore, because she kept falling asleep and missing huge chunks, and I would have to re-read whole pages when she woke up.

And then the Squirrel came. That was how I thought of him, because he had such bright eyes and bobbing ways, and such a fine fluffy beard. When he was in a good mood he made me laugh out loud, but usually he just kept me working and working. Latin, Arithmetic, Geometry, Algebra, History, Music. I like Geography. I like turning the great globe of the world and tracing the routes to the countries that Father has visited. India. China. America. I have a glass case full of huge shells from the Indian Ocean and the Pacific Ocean. When I hold them to my ear I can hear the sea in them, great booms of the waves of thousands of miles away.

My father has a Great Plan. One day he is going to sail to Australia, in his own ship. While it is being built we have a model of it in the schoolroom. I have made seamen and passengers to place on the decks – I even have a ship's cat running up a ladder! It has a cricket deck and a ballroom with crystal chandeliers; my father says it is a floating palace. And this is the best thing – it is going to be called the *Liverpool Lady*. That was my idea. And it will be the finest ship in the world.

Every day, I have luncheon with my sisters and the Squirrel in the dining room, four of us at a table that can seat twelve. We have cold mutton and boiled potatoes, and sometimes the Squirrel reads aloud to us while we eat. Caroline watches him all the time he is reading, and sometimes a slow, red blush creeps up out of his collar and rises to the top of his head. I wonder if she is waiting for him to make mistakes. I can't imagine any other reason for her interest.

But after the meal is finished my own trial begins. Hollins brings in a rod on a silver platter, and he and Timothy the footman help me to slip my jacket off and then put it back on with the rod lodged across my shoulder blades. Victoria looks on without a smile.

'I hate it, Victoria,' I moan.

'Never mind. It will hold your back straight. When you can stand as stiff and straight as Father, then you can stop wearing it.'

How I hate that rod! I have to wear it for a whole hour, and every second brings more discomfort. I cannot sit down, so must wander round the great house with it, doing my best to stride like my father. I can hear Caroline playing the piano, tripping out wrong notes and crashing chords with great gusto. The Squirrel moons around outside the drawing room, trying to hum along with her. Victoria goes to lie down, and I am left to my torture.

My shoulders hurt. My head aches because of the morning's lessons in a stuffy room, and I only have an hour to myself before I have to start again. I walk up and down along the draughty corridors with their gilt-framed paintings of my grandfathers and their grandfathers. They were a gloomy lot. At the end of the corridor there is a painting of my mother holding me in her arms. I am six months old there. She died when I was eight years old. I have no other picture of her beyond this young, gently smiling woman in the painting, who never grows older, never moves or speaks or laughs. When I come to a window I stare out at the lawns where the gardeners are working. One of the boys is about my age. I can sometimes hear him whistling.

I like to go down the main stairs where more of my gloomy ancestors are hanging, and then down again to the servants' door. On our side the door is a deep rosewood, and it has a sparkling crystal knob that catches the lights of all the lamps when they are lit. On the other side the door is covered in green baize, like the billiard table in the games room. When I was a little boy I used to love to open the door and run the back of my hand along the fluffy baize. The knob on that side is plain brass, and the stairs leading down are uncarpeted.

When I hear laughter coming from down below I know that is because Bains is out of the way upstairs supervising the arranging of flowers in the drawing room, in case my sisters have afternoon visitors. I long to slip downstairs like I used to do when I was little, and sit listening to the kitchen gossip. Joan used to push a warm pastry crust across the table to me, with a secret look that told me to eat it up and keep quiet. She was Nanny's sister, and every bit as large and loving as she was. But Nanny has gone now. I am too old for Nanny, Victoria said. I had to have the weeping governess and the fidgety Squirrel instead of Nanny.

Sometimes as I hesitate there on the top step I hear a slight cough and turn to see Hollins behind me.

'Did you want something, Master George?'

'No, thank you, Hollins. It's quite all right.'

'Ring your bell if you need me.'

'Of course.'

I stand back and Hollins goes through the door, and he is about to close it behind him when I say, 'Actually, I just wondered, Hollins. Is the rocking horse still in the cellar?'

Hollins remains with his gloved hand on the brass knob, and is so deeply silent that I wonder whether he has heard me at all. Then, with the slightest nod of his head, he says, 'I believe the rocking horse is still there, Master George.'

The door closes, and the house is silent again. Caroline reaches her last crashing chord on the piano and goes to her room to read. It is time for afternoon lessons to start. I climb up the stairs past the ancestors, and up to the top floor, to the schoolroom which used to be my nursery, to the table by the window where my old rocking horse used to stand.

My bedroom is next door. One night, the night after Nanny left, I woke up and came into the nursery, lonely and sad, missing her. And my rocking horse had gone.

The Day I Spoke to Master George

Ma's friend, Wiley, was Miss Caroline's maid, and she used to tell Ma that it was a miserable household, not like when Ma used to work there. But things seemed to perk up a lot when the new tutor came. She told Ma that everybody below stairs called him the Squirrel, because he fidgeted so much. The other thing that she said about him was that he was madly in love with Miss Caroline! Can you imagine that?

We only ever heard things like that from Wiley, and then we had to strain to listen because her voice would drop right down to a mumble when she was talking Big House news. Pa never said very much about the House to us, in fact he never said much to us at all, and Ma never repeated what she heard to him or to us, but when Wiley came visiting she would bring an hour's worth of whispered gossip with her. That's how we knew so much about Master George. We looked forward to Wiley's visits as much as Ma did, and giggled silently at the long words she used.

'The Squirrel is infatuated,' she announced when she

came to tea, spraying cake crumbs as she spoke. 'But Caroline is unassailable.'

We stored up the words like treasures to be brought out from time to time. 'Aren't you just infatuated with these roast spuds?' I used to say during Sunday dinner, but never if Pa was there. We weren't allowed to speak at table, ever, never mind giggle.

'Yes, but the dumplings are unassailable,' Walter would answer. Harry would raise his eyebrows at us as if he thought we were incredibly childish, but I have an idea that he was jealous because he didn't know words like that. Anyway, according to Wiley, Master George had his meals in the great dining room of the Big House with wicked Miss Victoria and dreamy Miss Caroline, eating spuds and cold meat, while the Squirrel read to them. Now that would give me hiccups! Pa had to stand at the door waiting for them to finish eating so he could signal to the servants to bring the next course. He wasn't allowed to look at the gentry, but he wasn't allowed to miss anything either. I think that was very clever.

So when we heard about him bringing a rod in every day for Master George's back, we were a bit shocked. But if Miss Victoria tells Pa to do something, he just has to do it. It wasn't him who told us though, or Wiley. It was Master George himself. I think it must have been the first time he was allowed out on his own. We must have been about eleven by then.

I was following Walter home from school that day. I was never allowed to play with his friends and I didn't

hey were all boys, and very noisy too.
of the butler on a neighbouring estate.
lt's, the shipping people. His hair was
red do anything, which usually meant
got the others into trouble while he shinned off
over a wall and escaped. No one really liked him. Bobby
was the coachman's son and little Moses lived in the
village shop near the school. I quite liked Moses.

But the mean thing was that, these days, when the
boys were playing out I had to go home and help Ma.
It wasn't fair, but there it was. So I used to follow them
sometimes, just to keep out of Ma's way, and that's what
happened that day. It was late March and all the daffodils
were out and the birds had their beaks full of bits of twigs
and sheep wool and leaves to make nests with. It was
much too nice to go home and darn stockings or make
bread or whatever it was that Ma would be expecting me
to do. I heard Rufus in his bossy barking voice daring the
others to go with him to the pond on our Estate and look
for frogspawn, and I thought, if Walter's brave enough,
then so am I.

The pond was in the wild part of the Estate, where you
could be quite sure the gentry wouldn't think of walking.
It was still out of bounds to us though. We had our own
playing area next to the field where Hercules grazed, and
we were lucky to have that, Ma said. If Rufus hadn't been
egging them on the boys would never, never have gone to
the pond, and neither would I.

I liked spying on them. I used to do it quite often. I'm

pretty sure Walter knew I was doing it, but he never gave me away. I dodged from tree to tree, just keeping them in sight, quick as a shadow. I could hear them whooping round the edge of the pond and splashing into the water, but I didn't go any closer. I didn't want to play any of their silly games anyway. Spying on them was much more fun.

I have to let you into a secret. I used to write it all down; everything. Everybody knew about Walter and his stories. If he didn't become a butler like Pa and Grandpa then he was going to be a famous writer one day. Everybody knew that. He made up fantastic adventure stories and showed them to Miss Brogan and sometimes he read them out to Ma.

'Where does it all come from, Walter?' Ma used to say. 'What a wonder you are!'

Well, I didn't tell anyone that I wrote things too. I didn't make things up like Walter. I just wrote about things that happened every day, round our Estate. That was my secret, and not even Walter knew about it. How could I be telling you all this if I hadn't been scribbling it down all those years ago? When Master George told me things I used to write it down exactly the way he said it. I can hear his voice now, just as it was when he was telling us about the rod in his jacket, and the night he lost his rocking horse. He had a posh voice, not like ours, and he sometimes made a little clicking sound behind his teeth when he was thinking. Yes, I can hear it now.

Tweeny couldn't read or write anyway, so I had to write

her bits just the way she talked too – a bit cocky, and a bit shy. I couldn't always understand her because she came from over the water, in Birkenhead. Wiley said she was common.

But I'm getting a bit ahead of myself. I hadn't spoken to Master George yet, had I, let alone Tweeny? And Tweeny hadn't even come to work at the Big House. Where was I? Oh yes! Hiding near the pond.

When the boys came past me again their clothes were all streaked with mud and their boots were squelching. They were carrying chipped mugs as carefully as if they were bone china, their faces frowning with concentration. Moses didn't have a mug. He danced sideways alongside them, his wet bootlaces flapping on the grass.

'Can't I have some?' he pleaded.

'No,' said Rufus. 'Get your own.'

'Ah, but I haven't got anything to carry them in.' He appealed to Walter. 'Can't you bring some round to our shop later? I'll give you an aniseed ball.'

'I said, get your own.' Rufus made his voice loud and rough, like a bulldog.

I felt sorry for Moses. They were all mean to him because he was the smallest.

'I'm going to come back and get that newt,' he muttered, and this time Walter swung on him, nearly spilling the contents of his mug.

'No you don't, Moses Ginsberg. That newt belongs to our Estate. You'd be stealing it if you took it.'

Moses ran off without saying goodbye, his face red and podged up with disappointment.

'He wouldn't dare pick that newt up anyway,' Bobby giggled. 'It's a whopper.'

'It'd bite his nose off,' Rufus said. 'I wouldn't even touch it.'

When their voices had died away I came out of the shelter of the rhododendrons. I had a little wooden box in my schoolbag that I kept my pens and pencils in. It had a sliding lid that had red flowers carved into it, and my name, Dorothy, in green. I loved it. I wondered about putting some frogspawn in it and giving it to Moses at school next day. I didn't know whether I dared, that was the trouble. Frogspawn was such slithery, floloppy stuff. Fancy picking it up in my hands! I ran down to the pond, which was almost hidden in the long grass beyond the orchard. I'd never been that far into the Estate before. I sat on the bank watching a brown duck being chased by two very smart jewelly ones, and knew I wouldn't want to wade into that sludgy pond looking for frogspawn. It didn't matter. It was lovely just being there.

Then I suddenly realized that I wasn't alone. You know that sensation you have when somebody's eyes are on you, and you go all prickly and self-conscious and you can't remember how to make your face go normal? I turned round after a bit. The boy from the Big House was standing watching me.

'Good afternoon, Master George.' I jumped up quick, ready to run back home if he told me off, but he just nodded to me and came nearer, whistling slightly between his teeth, just like Walter did sometimes when he was nervous, and he stood with his hands in his pockets watching the ducks.

'Mallards. They're courting, you know,' he said. 'That's why they're chasing each other like that.'

I giggled. 'She can't be bothered with them, can she? Fly away, Miss Mallard, while you have the chance!'

'She'll have to marry one of them though. It's nature, that is.'

'Is it?'

'Everyone gets married some time.'

'Miss Victoria didn't.' I was embarrassed, that's why that came out. Funny how words just pop out of your mouth sometimes, as if they've got nothing to do with you. I wanted to swallow them back again, but it was too late, he'd heard me.

'Ah. That's because no one wanted her.'

I risked a sideways glance at Master George. I wondered if he knew that all the servants called Miss Victoria 'the wicked sister'. Best not to mention it, I decided.

Master George chuckled. He had a nice laugh. He picked up a little branch and flung it into the water and as it splashed down all three mallards flapped their wings in alarm, churning up the water and then lifting themselves up and away out of sight beyond the orchard. I stared after them and then turned away. There was no reason to stay now the ducks had gone. There was nothing to talk about.

'She's not very nice,' George went on. 'And she's plain. Not like you.' He was still staring at the pond. 'I should think you'll get married.'

'I don't want to.' I could feel myself blushing now. 'I want to be a lady's maid, like Ma used to be.'

'Oh well, you won't then. Servants aren't allowed to get married.'

'Pa did.'

'But he's the butler. Caroline says he's one in a million, your father.' And as he said it his voice faltered. 'A jolly good butler, and his father before him, I believe.'

'That's what Walter's going to do too,' I said, 'but Wiley says he'll have to learn discretion first.'

'What does that mean?'

'I don't know.'

'It may be something to do with polishing the silver.'

We were quiet again. I wondered if it was all right to stay there now Master George had finished speaking to me. On the other hand, he hadn't dismissed me.

'I might have to go home for my tea,' I said.

Master George crouched down to have a closer look at the pond, and as he did so something slithered past his boot, startling him. 'I say!'

'It's that newt!' I crouched down next to him, trailing my skirt hem in the mud. 'It's a whopper, Bobby said. I heard the boys nattering about it . . .' I stopped suddenly, remembering that the boys had been trespassing when they came to the pond, just as I was.

'Would you like it?' Master George asked me.

I stared at him, not knowing what to say, and without taking off his boots or socks he ploughed into the water and stood with his hands on his hips, peering down through the thick sweep of yellow hair that had fallen across his face.

'There he goes!' he shouted, wading in up to his knees. Suddenly he plunged his hands into the water and came up with the newt wriggling in his grasp. He held it high above his head. 'Got him!' he shouted, triumphant. He splashed back to the bank, holding the newt out towards me. 'Here. He's yours.'

I must say I didn't really want to touch the thing. It was all glistening and twisty, as black as coal. Master George turned it round and I could see its spotty yellow underbelly. He tucked it under one arm and fished in his pocket to find a handkerchief. 'Here. Spread this out.'

I did as I was told, fumbling in my nervousness, and Master George knelt down and rolled up the newt in it. Then he placed it in my arms.

'Come and play tomorrow,' he said. 'My new tutor's a great sport. He doesn't mind at all if I want to play out.'

I hugged my damp parcel to my chest and ran home, giggling and proud. I was a bit frightened of the way the newt plunged about to be free and kept twisting its head up to look at me. I was desperate not to drop it. I kept my eyes fixed on it as I stumbled along. 'I won't hurt you,' I kept whispering to it. 'Come on, newty. You'll be all right.' I didn't stop running until I reached the cottage.

Walter was sitting on the outside step polishing the boots for next day. It was his punishment for coming home covered in mud. He was talking to himself as he brushed, trying to make himself work faster so he could run off and play again. He always does that. He reckons it helps. He was so impatient, that was his trouble.

'Walter, open the gate,' I panted, nearly crying with excitement. 'I've got the newt. I've got the newt!'

He dropped his brushes and ran to me, and then stopped at the gate, gazing in awe at the flailing newt in my arms. Harry jumped down from the bedroom window on to the flat half-roof over the door, and down again on to the lawn. He whistled.

'Crikey, what a monster!' he said. 'It's an emperor, did you know that?'

They both danced round me, waving their arms and demanding to have a turn at holding the newt, but I shouted back at them to keep still and stop frightening it. I refused to let go.

'No, it's mine. Master George gave it me.'

'Just give me a go of it,' Walter pleaded. 'Just for half a minute.'

Ma came out to see what was going on, took one look at the newt and flapped her dish cloth at it.

'You're not bringing that thing into the house. Let it go, Dorothy Hollins. This minute.'

Oh, Ma! Reluctantly, I lowered the newt down to the ground. At once it squirmed out of its handkerchief and slithered off into the grass. Walter picked up a stone to fling after it. I think he was just excited, that's why he did that.

'Drop that!' Ma said, in a quiet voice that was just meant for him, and he froze, his wrist still cocked back.

'I'm surprised at you, Walter. Who was it won the Sunday school prize for nature study *only last week*? And here you are, chucking stones at an innocent creature!'

He turned away from her, his face blazing with shame. I felt guilty for him. I could feel my own face burning, but it was my turn next.

'And as for you, Dorothy . . . look at the state of you! I've never seen you looking such a mess! Your pinafore covered in mud – and your boots, and your sleeves! I've spent the whole day out here scrubbing the washing and here you are bringing me more already! Whatever were you thinking of, the pair of you?'

Harry had sneaked back to the house and hoisted himself up on to the flat roof, where he sat cross-legged like an imp, laughing at us. Ma turned to him and he streaked back through the bedroom window. She turned back to me.

'And whose is this handkerchief, might I ask?'

'Master George's.' I daren't look at Walter. I knew I would giggle if I did. I could feel him shaking beside me.

'Lord, if I haven't got enough to do without doing his washing as well. Master George's handkerchief! Whatever next?'

As she turned away from us I was sure I caught just the flicker of a smile across her face. She once said, just out of nowhere one night when we were all sitting reading by the fire, that if there was one person she felt sorry for on the entire Estate, it was the young master, without a friend in the world, and never allowed out on his own. But that half-sad, half-pleased smile didn't last for long. She swung right back to us with: 'Get upstairs both of you, out of those clothes, and into bed.'

We lay on top of our bed watching the dance of leaf shadow on the ceiling. Somewhere outside a blackbird was pouring its heart out. We could hear the distant voices of the labourers working in the fields.

'It was a lovely newt,' I said.

'We could have sold it to Moses.'

'It was mine though. Master George said I could have it.'

'Fancy him giving you a newt. Just like that.'

'He wants to be friends.'

Walter said nothing. Neither of us had ever spoken to Master George before. We'd seen him riding in the carriage with his sisters, or walking round the Estate, hands behind his back and his head held slightly to one side, just like his father.

'I hate going to bed early,' I said.

'I know. I hadn't finished playing out. I hadn't actually started.'

'We haven't even had tea!'

We heard the sound of Pa's boots on the path, and his chair scraping on the floor as he sat down for his rest. Then we could hear the familiar faint crackling sound of brass-band music. He was given half an hour a day to spend with his family and he always spent it the same way, listening to music. He would wind up his great horned gramophone and listen to a record. No one was allowed to speak while the record was on. He would sit upright with his head lolling on the back of his chair and his eyes closed. We always used to think he'd dropped off to sleep, except for the minute, steady tap, tap, tap of one finger in time to the music. But if any of us made the slightest sound he would open his eyes and glare at us.

Even upstairs we lay there without saying a word while the record was playing. Walter's fingers tiptoed under the bed for his story book and pencil and he began to scribble. I could just about read the words 'The Monster in the Pond' before his hand cupped over it.

'Go on,' I whispered. 'Read it me.'

'The monster had scales like the teeth on a giant saw. Green blood dripped from its mouth,' he wrote. 'It was as big as a horse, and fire steamed from its nostrils. Its eyes flashed sparks as it swung its head round to look at Dorothea. As she turned to run away it grabbed her round the neck with its steely talons. Poor Dorothea's screams could be heard as far away as Mossley Hill church. Then, just as she was going under the green, scummy water, the brave young Will Tanner came swinging down from a tree . . . I'm a bit stuck now.'

If we were allowed to burn a candle Walter would probably read it all to me later in his best scary voice, and it would be so exciting that we would both have a nightmare.

At last the record downstairs finished and Pa's chair

squeaked as he stood up to go back to work. He wouldn't be home again until the gentry and all the servants had gone to bed, and all the candles and lamps of the Big House had been snuffed out. As soon as he had gone we could hear Ma talking, and Harry came upstairs with a plate of sandwiches and some warm, jammy scones. He sat on the edge of our bed eating half of them.

'I'll take you fishing on Saturday,' he promised Walter. 'Fish are better than newts any day. You can eat fish.'

He fetched a comic from under his mattress and he and Walter sat giggling over it until it was too dark to see any more. I lay looking at the ghostly moon and thinking about the newt, hoping it would be able to find its way back to the pond, and trying to imagine how the young Will Tanner could possibly save me from its grasp.

Our Favourite Tree

The next day, Walter and I didn't have to say anything about it to each other, we just knew what we were going to do. We didn't mention it to Rufus or the others. It was nothing to do with them any more. After school we just made straight for the Estate pond, and there was Master George waiting for us.

I was suddenly eaten up with shyness. 'Hello, Master George,' I said. Walter tried to say the same but his tongue stuck in his throat. He slapped the side of his leg as Miss Brogan always told him to do when he couldn't get going.

Master George nodded to us and clicked behind his teeth. I could tell he was a bit shy too, and full of smiles inside like we were, but trying really hard not to show it.

'Ma wouldn't let me keep the newt,' I said.

Master George nodded. 'I expect he's splashing about in here then. We might see him.'

'Do you like fer-fer-fishing, Master George?' Walter got out at last.

'Never done it,' said Master George. 'Wouldn't mind trying though.'

'Me and our Harry are go-going on Saturday after-afternoon,' Walter gasped. It was a huge sentence for him to get out when he was so nervous, and nothing else would come after that. He gave up talking and started shovelling up little stones with the toe of his boot.

'Walter was wondering if you'd like to go with them,' I blurted out, when I realized how hopeless it all seemed.

Master George looked at Walter and then looked away again. His eyes were full of light. 'S'posed to have lessons, but I think my tutor might let me. He's a jolly good sort.'

'The Squirrel,' I said, and we all spluttered.

'Yes, I call him that too.' Master George looked surprised. 'Have you seen him?'

'No. We just know his name.'

We had to laugh out loud then. We couldn't help it. I think it was a way of letting out all the tension. Master George did an imitation of the Squirrel twitching about in his chair, and then Walter scooped up a pebble and sat on his haunches, clutching it in both hands and pretending to nibble it as if it was a nut, his cheeks all pouched up. Master George was doubled up with laughter.

'Would you l-like to climb our tree?' Walter asked, much encouraged.

'I'll say!'

Walter set off at a run and Master George loped after him, up through the orchard and across the forbidden lawns. I started to run after them and then gave up. I was angry and upset. I was the one who had spoken to him first. He was my friend. And now Walter had stolen him. It wasn't fair. I trailed after them slowly, and just stood there while Walter showed him our favourite tree, the sailing ship tree. I wasn't allowed to climb it, you see. Ma wouldn't let me. It wasn't fair.

I could see Walter shinning up it without any difficulty. He knew the routes. He sat straddling a branch waiting for Master George to follow. I must say he made an awfully bad job of it. At first he kept slipping back and grazing his knees, but he was quite determined to get to the top. I stood below coaxing and shoving and Walter shouted encouragement and advice from above, and at last he managed to clamber on to the branch, red-faced and panting, and haul himself up next to Walter.

'Look at the world!' Walter said, sweeping his arm round.

'You can even see outside the Estate!' Master George said.

'You can see another country!' Walter stood up, clinging on to a higher branch and edging himself along. 'That's Wales over there.'

'Where the wizards live,' George said. 'Gosh!'

'And – and dragons,' said Walter.

'I want to go to Wales one day,' I called up.

Their faces peered down at me like balloons.

George stood up nervously, holding on to a higher branch like Walter and scanning the horizon. 'My father has been all round the world. I shall, one day. I'll probably take my butler with me, Walter.'

'I might not want to ber-be a ber-butler.' Walter's stammer had come back. He swung himself back down the tree, awkward now, losing his grip and sliding part of the way. He was showing off. He laughed to show he wasn't hurt, though he was. He sat nursing his arm, waiting for Master George to join him.

'You could go to China!' he called up. 'They have dragons there too.'

'I say, it's a lot easier coming down than going up,' Master George said. His feet lolloped above my head and I grabbed his ankles and guided them back to the trunk. He came down in a flurry of leaves and twigs, scarlet faced and triumphant.

'I'd like to go round the world. I'll be your wife's maid,' I said. 'And I'm sure we could talk Walter round, Master George.'

'I'll have to go back now. Lessons, you know. I'm supposed to be doing Algebra. I'll have to make sure Victoria doesn't see me,' Master George said, standing up at last and shaking grass off his torn trousers. He gave a funny little cough and squinted his eyes as if the sun was too bright all of a sudden. 'I say, that was awfully good fun, you know.'

He loped towards the drive, and Walter cupped his hands round his mouth to shout after him.

'See you at the g-gates on Saturday. Half-past-two.'

'Which gates? Servants' or gentry?' I prompted.

'Gentry, of course,' Walter said. 'We'll be on the outside.'

'Do you really think he'll be there?' I wondered.

We didn't tell Ma that Master George would be coming, and we decided to keep it a secret from Harry too, so it would be a surprise. We could think of nothing else for the rest of the week. But, of course, when Saturday came round I was forbidden to go on the fishing trip. It seemed like the end of the world when Ma told me I couldn't go.

'No, it's out of the question,' Ma said when I tried to plead with her. 'Girls don't go fishing. I thought you'd learnt your lesson over that blessed newt.'

And it was no use arguing. Ma wouldn't change her mind, and she found a job for me mending Harry's old playing-out clothes so Walter could wear them when he grew a bit. And then in the end it wasn't a fishing trip either, because Harry was asked to work some extra hours that afternoon, and he wouldn't lend out his rods to Walter.

'But Master George is coming!' Walter protested, letting out the secret at last, but Harry didn't believe him anyway. He just winked at him, which was his annoying new way of showing us how grown-up he was, and cycled off to work. So Walter pretended he was going for a walk on the cast-iron shore at Dingle, where all the bits of scrap metal got washed in by the river. And that afternoon, something really awful happened.

Dorothy

Yes! I Did It!

*W*alter told me all about it later, and I knew that it was true and that he hadn't made a word of it up.

I was mending Harry's clothes, as I said. I really don't know how he managed to get his breeches in such a state. I spent a good hour darning patches on and I could have cried with frustration, because it was such a lovely afternoon outside and our cottage was so dark and damp by comparison. Ma had let the fire go out because she wanted to clean the oven, and I was shivering and sniffing and driving her mad, I think.

'You have to learn,' she said. 'Women are the workers in this world.'

'I never want to be a woman then,' I said. 'I don't want to grow up. Anyway, I bet Miss Caroline and Miss Victoria don't darn old clothes.'

'What they do and don't do has nothing to do with us,' Ma said, scrubbing away in rhythm to her words. 'They were born different, and that's that.'

I tried to think about this, but it didn't make sense. Because they were rich, they didn't have to do jobs. Because I was a girl, I couldn't go out and play on a Saturday afternoon.

Was it like that all over the world? I felt something fizzing up in my head as if I'd swallowed too much sherbet. I took Harry's mended breeches upstairs and put them in the clothes chest. I'd made a good job of them, and I was proud of that. Then I closed the lid and went downstairs. Ma had her back to me, reaching up the flue of the stove with her spiky black brush, and without saying anything to her I went outside.

The warm wind rushed around me and all the bright daffodils were nodding in the grass. Little clouds rolled across the sky as if they were lambs chasing one another across a field. I suddenly felt so happy and free that I wanted to shout out loud. I'd finished my job, and I'd done it well, and now the rest of the day was going to be mine.

I ran over to Hercules's fence and he came trotting over to me and slapped his great lips together asking for grass.

'Silly,' I laughed, 'yours is just as good.'

But I pulled up a handful for him and he rolled back his wet lips and sucked it out of my palm. I stood up on the fence and clambered on to his back, and he trotted peacefully round for a bit and then sloped his neck right down so I rolled off. He hated being ridden. He was Mawks's pony, and his job was to mow the great lawns of the Estate, pulling a huge roller behind him. He had to wear leather boots when he did that so he didn't damage the lawns with his hooves. But today he was free. We were both free.

I climbed on to his back again and he set off at a trot

this time, straight for the trees. I knew what was in his mind. His plan was to trot under a branch so it would knock me off, but I steadied myself just as I'd seen Walter doing. I knew what to do. The trick was to stay on board for as long as you dared. I could still have rolled off into the long grass, but I egged him on. 'Come on, Hercules! Come on, boy!' And I dug the heels of my boots into him to make him go faster. I was bumping up and down till I had no breath left, but I wouldn't give in. If Walter could do it, so could I.

I kept my eyes fixed on the bottom branch of the chestnut tree. 'Go on, Hercules!' I shouted. Just when it seemed that the time had come to throw myself off him I flung up my arms instead and yes! I did it! As we reached the branch I lifted myself up by my elbows and clung on to it. Hercules trotted on, riderless, and very pleased with himself. And I was pleased with myself too. I'd always wanted to do that.

So there I was, hanging from the very branch that Master George had hung from the other day. I could have let go and landed on the grass without hurting myself. But instead I swung my legs right up and crisscrossed my knees over the branch. If Ma could have seen me! I edged towards the trunk of the tree and swung myself round until I was sitting on the branch. There below was Hercules grazing the sweet grass that he loved. 'Hello, Hercules!' I called. He flicked his ears and looked up at me and rolled his eyes as if to say, 'Stuck up a tree, are you? Let that be a lesson to you!'

But I wasn't stuck. I was exactly where I wanted to be. After a bit, when I'd got my breath back and stopped shaking, I made myself stand up on the branch, clinging with both arms to the trunk, and I looked up into my sailing ship tree. Branches spread out above me like spars, and behind the fluttering canopy of leaves the sky was as blue as the ocean. I reached up and grasped the branch above me and levered myself up. My pinafore was such a nuisance. The pocket snagged on a twig and I heard it rip.

'Don't worry, Ma, I'll mend it,' I said to myself. I wasn't going to give up now. How could I? I stretched and clambered, stretched and clambered, feeling my way with the tips of my fingers, and every time I looked up the sun glinted through the leaves, and every time I looked down my stomach swirled. At last I was below Walter's branch. I couldn't reach it. It was impossible. I made myself dizzy and sick with the effort. How did he do it? He was exactly the same height as me, and yet he climbed on to it easily. I made one last effort, and then I saw it, a little notch just big enough to fit the toe of my boot into. Now I could scramble up.

I sat on his branch and looked at the world. All around me the branches swayed and danced and the spring-green leaves spiralled. The flowers of the white candles were just beginning to burst open. And beyond them, I could see our cottage. I watched Ma coming out to the end of the garden with her hands on her hips, and I knew she was looking for me. I could see the Big House with all its windows glimmering in the sunlight. I thought of Pa walking up and down all the stairs all day and sitting down to rest his feet in the cosy pantry, and the yellow canary singing to him. I could see a team of horses pulling a plough across a brown field, and beyond that, the gleaming river and the ships busy on it. And I could see the purple-green hills of Wales, just as Walter had described them. It was mine, all this. I'd won it by my own effort.

There was a hole in the trunk of the tree, just above my branch, and I stuck my hand in it and brought out a little tin box. I opened it up and inside it was a black leather notebook. I knew what it was. I opened it up, and there in his scrawly writing Walter had written 'The Amazing Adventures of Young Will Tanner by Walter Hollins. Book One'. I knew all these stories. I opened up one of the pages, and started to read out loud.

'The Green Giant of Moel Famau. All alone he stood, the young Will Tanner, and faced the Green Giant of Moel Famau. Behind him the people of his village cowered and prayed. His old mother called out to him, "Save us, Will! Only you can do it!" Will held up his hand, and from nowhere appeared a golden falcon, and settled on his wrist. "Trust me," the falcon said, in a voice that only Will could hear.'

I turned over the page. Far away, someone was calling my name.

' "If I slay you, your people will die!" the Green Giant said, and his voice rumbled like thunder and made the houses crumble into dust. "And I will slay you if you don't give me the fair Dorothea for my bride. Step aside, swain." '

I closed the book. I knew the rest by heart. Dorothea lay swooning beside her brother. Will did not turn aside, but advanced one step, two, three, while the Giant drew himself up to his full height and laughed him to scorn. And then Will held up his arm and shouted, 'Strike!' The golden falcon flew at the giant and gashed out his eyes and the blood spurted from them like a crimson fountain and the giant fell in a heap on the ground. Will drew his sword and cut off the giant's head, and turning, gave it to his sister.

Oh, it was a wonderful story!

I put the book in its box and pushed it back into the hole. Ma had stopped calling me and had gone back into the cottage. I was feeling very sleepy, the swaying leaves and the rocking tree and the scudding clouds seemed to be swirling me away, away from myself as if I was drifting out towards the sun.

A sudden shriek of a ship's hooter startled me. I stood up, straining to see through the curled leaves and the branches. Something went cold inside me, made the skin of my back prickle. I knew that there was a terrible danger out there, and that it was something to do with Walter. And, much later, I found out what it was.

Dorothy

It Was a Losing Battle

*M*aster George was waiting at the huge wrought-iron gates that let the horses and carriages into the Estate. At first he pretended not to see Walter running along the road from the servants' gate, and then he waved to him and walked up to meet him.

'You made it then. Good-oh!'

'Coming to the Cazzie?'

They ran down together towards the cast-iron shore. Out on the river rusty old dredgers were trailing their chains of buckets, scooping up silt. Sailing ships and chugging steamers were making their way to Garston Docks.

'Know what's in those ships?' Walter asked. There was no sign of his stammer today, and he felt full of himself; in charge.

'Pit-props,' Master George suggested, remembering something the Squirrel had told him, but Walter shook his head.

'Gold then.'

'That's only sometimes. Usually it's great bunches of bananas. And know what's in those bananas?'

Master George shook his head.

'Tranterlers. Great black spiders that eat men whole.'

'Tarantulas.' Master George corrected him.

'That's what I said.'

George stood with his hand shading his eyes, scanning the horizon. 'They could be my father's ships.'

'Is he a sailor?' Walter asked.

'No. He owns a shipping line.'

Walter knew that, but he was disappointed all the same. It was much more exciting to be a sailor, he was sure of that. 'I might be a sailor when I grow up, if I don't be a butler. Can't wait.'

But Master George wasn't listening. He ran ahead, kicking up sprays of grey sand like a horse that's been set free.

Walter ran after him, proud, wanting to show him everything. He was half-wishing that he'd asked Rufus and Bobby along so he could show off his new friend to them, but it was better this way. It was special. He could take Master George to all the best places, just as Harry did when they were out together.

'Can you do this?' he shouted. He picked up a handful of pebbles and lobbed them one by one into the water. They counted the bounces.

'Excellent!' said Master George. 'Show me how you do it.'

It seemed that he would never tire of it, once he'd got the hang of it, tipping his arm back and flicking his wrist just right so the stone skimmed and bounced across the surface. The gulls wheeled around them, thinking the tiny splashes the stones made were fish bobbing up to be eaten. Then all of a sudden Master George dropped his last fistful and put his hands in his pockets, bored.

'What about this fishing?'

'We can't fer-fish without tack-tackle,' Walter said. He was feeling a bit desperate now, in case Master George thought he'd let him down and would want to go back home and sit in his school room instead. He picked up a long skein of seaweed and wrapped it round his neck as if it was a scarf. Master George did the same.

'I know where there's a ber-boat. Only don't tell anyone.'

This was exactly what Harry had said a week ago, and he had added, 'If you do, Walter, you'll die a lingering death in a rock pool, nibbled up by crabs.' Walter had solemnly promised not to tell. But then, Harry had let him down over the fishing tackle. They ran side by side until eventually they found what they were looking for – a pale blue rowing boat complete with oars, pulled up well beyond the high tide mark. *Polly*, it was called.

'Here she is! The good ship *Polly*! We could row to China in her!'

They circled round it, whistling softly as if it was full of pieces of gold.

'What d'you think, Master George?'

'If the owner spots us we could just row down river and ditch it.'

'We wouldn't be stealing. Just having fun.'

They took their boots and socks off and put them

inside the boat, and then dragged it across the sand and mud until they reached the water. They scrambled in, whooping with delight as the boat bobbed free.

'You row, Walter.'

Walter picked up the oars and rowed clumsily, sending feathers of spray into the boat. Master George stripped off his jacket and shirt and sat in his vest, hugging himself. Water dappled round them, sparkling in sunlight.

'I can see why you want to be a sailor. It's a grand life, isn't it?'

Walter shipped the oars and pulled off his own jumper. He was wet through anyway. 'Watch out for pirates!' he sang out.

'Head for China,' Master George said. He stood up suddenly in the boat, causing it to rock wildly, and stripped off his trousers, flinging them into the soggy pile of clothes at the bottom of the boat. 'Might go for a dip,' he said.

'I wouldn't.' Walter was alarmed. 'Look how fast the tide's flowing.'

But Master George took no notice. He dived overboard and was immediately caught in the current and carried away towards the centre of the river. Walter leaned over the side of the boat, desperate to catch hold of him, but Master George was quickly well beyond his reach. He sat up and heaved on the oars. The distance between them was increasing. He was pulling as hard as he could, but it was a losing battle. Master George's dark head bobbed and sank, his arms flailing uselessly.

'Do something!' he yelled.

'I can't!'

At that moment there was an ear-splitting shriek, and Walter turned his head to see a steam ship bearing rapidly down on him. He tugged again at the oars, trying to turn the *Polly* round and head back to shore before he was ploughed down. He could see Master George's bobbing head in the river and knew that the ship would cleave the water between them like an axe cleaving through a tree. He crouched in his bobbing shell of a boat and waited for the end of the world to happen. Men on the ship shouted abuse at him, shaking their fists, and he cupped his hands round his mouth and yelled at the top of his voice.

'There's a ber-boy in the water. Look the other side, look the other side.'

But his small voice couldn't be heard above the noise of the ship and the shouts of the men. He was slammed from side to side of his boat as it wallowed in the wash.

At last the waters settled. With dread in his heart he peered over the side, and there, unbelievably, was Master George, still visible and floundering helplessly in the choppy waters. Walter couldn't believe he was still alive, but knowing that he was seemed to give him the strength he needed. He heaved on the oars till he felt his back would break with the effort, and at last he pulled up alongside him. They were both exhausted, but somehow Walter managed to lean right over and grasp Master George under the arms and haul him into the boat without capsizing it.

They slumped back into the boat, completely spent. Master George looked ghastly. He started coughing and a jet of water spewed from his mouth, and at last he opened his eyes.

'Gosh!' he said. 'Gosh, Walter. That was pretty close.' He struggled to sit up and gave him a sickly grin. 'Maybe I shouldn't have gone for a dip, after all.'

Walter couldn't speak. He was shaking all over, his hands and his legs, his whole body was shuddering as if his skin had come loose and he couldn't control it. All he could think of was what he would have done if he'd had to go home without Master George that day. He imagined going up to the Big House and telling Miss Victoria. Telling her what? That Master George had drowned in the River Mersey? He could feel great choking sobs rising up in him, and he couldn't hold them back.

'Here, don't do that,' said Master George. He scrambled forward awkwardly and sat next to Walter. 'How about getting on to dry land?' And even though he had never done anything for himself before in his life, he picked up one of the oars and dabbled about with it, and Walter dabbled with the other, and at last they summoned up enough strength between them to land on Grassendale shore. They hauled the boat up on to the sand and ditched it there.

Master George wrung out his shirt and trousers and put them on. They clung to him like wet paper.

'Gosh. Bit damp, these.'

He picked up the seaweed scarf and flicked it round

his neck, then he flapped his arms up and down so spray showered off him. He and Walter jogged round on the grassy bank to try and get warm again, then set off at a sprint towards the cast-iron shore, with their soggy boots bumping round their necks.

'Wonder if that ship was full of tarantulas?' Master George panted, and for some reason it was all suddenly hysterically funny. They couldn't even run for laughing. They toppled over and lay doubled up and helpless, their legs kicking up into the air, screaming like seagulls.

Just Remember Who Your Friends Are

You can imagine what Ma said when Walter squelched into the house. He was stripped of his wet clothes and sent straight to bed, and of course I was already there because of my torn pinafore and scratched arms and legs. I only got as far as admitting to Ma that I'd been riding Hercules, so the sailing ship tree was still my secret. I told Walter though, and he agreed that I should climb it as much as I wanted to now. And then I told him about hearing the shriek of the steamboat.

'It was something to do with you, wasn't it, Walter?'

'I suppose so.'

'And Master George?'

And out it came bit by bit, the terrible story of how Master George nearly got drowned. I knew every word of it was true. But it wasn't long before Walter reached for his new black notebook and was turning the story into another Will Tanner adventure.

'A pirate ship bore down on the young Prince George and brave Will Tanner. Its sails were black, and the pennant of a skull and crossbones fluttered from the mast, and it was called the *Scarlet Tarantula*. With howls of glee the jeering pirates fished poor, drowning Prince George out of the sea. They held a flashing dagger across his throat, and shouted out to young Will Tanner, "Bring us a ransom of ninety golden guineas, or he dies at sunset!" "Save me, Will!" the young price gasped. "Save me." The sea around Will's tiny boat was snapping with sharks . . .'

I think I fell asleep at that point.

Next day was Sunday, and we were both worrying when we woke up. Walter was worrying about the solo he was supposed to be singing at church that night. He hadn't told Ma or Pa because he wanted it to be a surprise for them, but the thing that was worrying him more than anything was the thought that he might start stammering in the middle of the anthem and get stuck. I just couldn't imagine how it could happen when he was singing, but he worried about it all the same.

And the thing that was worrying me was the thought that Master George must have had to tell Miss Victoria how his clothes got wet. What if she punished him? What if she made him tell her that he was with Walter when it happened? And then I thought of something even worse.

'Pa might lose his job,' I said.

Ma was always telling us that if we ever got into trouble at the Big House then the whole family would have to leave.

'She wouldn't have any mercy. Not that one,' I said, in Ma's voice exactly.

'It wasn't my fault he decided to go for a swim.'

'It doesn't matter. You weren't even supposed to be in that boat, Walter.'

It was raining all day, and we had to stay in. I knew Walter was dying to climb the tree and practise singing his anthem up there. Instead he had to stay in and play dominoes with Harry while I helped Ma to cook the dinner. We were both so fidgety that Walter upset the dominoes twice just when they'd got a really good run going, and I nearly put salt in the apple pie instead of sugar. Ma just caught me in time, and whisked the salt jar out of my hand. She was in a good mood though, and only laughed about it.

'The first time I baked a pudding,' she told me, 'my ma told me to put a whole egg in, and I did! Still in its shell! I was never allowed to forget that! But I don't know what Pa would have said to a salty apple pie. He loves his Sunday pie.'

Sunday was the one day of the week when Pa sometimes ate with us. We had to wait until the gentry had finished eating their meal and all the washing done and all the silver put away, and then he would come home. We would listen for him humming as he came through our gate, and then Ma would whisk the cooking pots and things off the table and float a clean white cloth across it, and Walter and I would set out the cutlery. It had to be done every bit as perfectly as at the Big House; both Ma and Pa were very particular about that.

But Pa wasn't humming that Sunday. He was very

quiet, even more inside himself than usual, but he didn't seem to be angry. We watched him anxiously. We couldn't work out his mood at all. He sat listening to sacred music on his gramophone while Ma stirred the juices of the meat into the gravy, and when the record was finished he was still sitting there with his eyes closed. Ma tapped him playfully on the shoulder and he brought his chair over to the table and rolled up his sleeves to carve the joint.

This was a wonderful thing to watch. First he sharpened the carving knife, flicking it from one side to the other so quickly that sparks flew from it, then he slid the knife into the side of the meat. While he carved the meat, Ma breathed out deeply, satisfied to see how well it was cooked. Our plates were passed down the table with the slices steaming on them, and then Pa said grace, and we all sat with our heads bowed and our eyes closed. And that Sunday he said a strange thing. He blessed the food, as usual, and then said, 'Let us be specially thankful for this day. Let us remember those who have been lost at sea.'

Walter groaned out loud, and Ma put her hand on his forehead.

'Are you ill?' she asked.

Walter shook his head. He was certainly very pale.

'He came home in damp clothes yesterday,' she said to Pa.

I don't think we took a breath, either of us, while Pa spooned roast potatoes and sprouts and apple sauce on to his plate and leaned forward slowly for the gravy boat, and Harry looked from one to the other of us, his mouth open and his eyes wicked with fun, even though he didn't know what had gone on yesterday. Now, surely, Pa would mention Master George and the state of his clothes.

'If he's caught a chill, he'd better not go to church,' Pa said, and we breathed out again. The conversation between them drifted on about a great ship called the *Titanic* that had sunk, and we looked at each other and pulled faces. Something wasn't right, but it didn't seem to be anything to do with the good ship *Polly*.

After the meal had been cleared away we put on our Sunday best for church. Pa looked every bit as smart as the gentry, and Ma wore the long black dress and hat that she had worn when she was a lady's maid. Walter persuaded them that he was well enough to go and had to put on his sailor suit, even though it would be covered up by his surplice when he was in church. He and Harry raced on ahead so they wouldn't be late for choir.

When they arrived, the stringy old choirmaster said that the verger had been taken sick and that there was no one to ring the church bell or wind the clock. Rufus McCartney volunteered straight away, and Mister Thorn peered at him suspiciously and sent Walter after him.

Rufus was going wild. He heaved on the bell rope, tugging it up and down so the great bell swung about like a drunken sailor. As soon as he let go, Walter heaved on it. They took it in turns, jumping as high as they could to grasp the rope, and with every swing of the bell they were pulled off their feet. *Diddydoing doing Diddy doing de doing. Doing. De diddy de diddy.* We heard it as we were walking across the fields and wondered what on earth was going on. It sounded as if knight in armour were chucking pans at each other.

'That'll do!' Mr Thorn roared up the stairwell. 'You're giving the crows a headache!'

'Beat you to the clock!' Rufus said. They ran up the winding stone staircase of the clock tower, tripping over their long red cassocks, round and round in total darkness, groping for the narrow stone steps in front of them and counting as they went. One hundred and nineteen would bring them to the top. Rufus stopped every now and again to make whooing ghost noises, and the echoes shivered into the eerie darkness. There was a rush of blinding light and they were standing on the wooden platform by the bells. The church bell had stopped its clanging and hung silent, swaying just gently, next to the five great clock bells.

'We have fun together, don't we, Walter?' Rufus asked, panting for breath.

'Yes, we do. It was grand that.'

Walter ran his finger over the great bell, reading aloud the letters that were inscribed into it.

"With loving voice I call to church and prayer,
And bid the living for the grave prepare. 1872."

'That'll have frightened half of 'em to death already,' he was saying, and suddenly Rufus had him by the shoulders and was pushing his head against the clock casing.

'Then why did you go off with that posh nob, eh? Aren't I good enough any more?'

'Stop it, Rufus. Let go, will you?'

'I'm your pal. You play with me on Saturday afternoons. I was standing round waiting for you. Then Bobby said you'd gone off with that toff.' With every sentence he banged Walter's head, then he threw him off as if he was disgusted with him. 'Just remember who your friends are in future.'

Walter turned away, trying not to show the tears of pain and surprise that welled up in him. He stood with his hands on his hips looking out at the green fields spreading in every direction, and the people like little dolls filing along the lanes.

'If I was a crow I'd fly away now.'

'I'll give you a push if you like,' Rufus said. 'Come on, get cranking.'

He opened the door of the clock mechanism and cranked the great key for the chime and the hour. It had been made by Mr Thomas Bellringer, who was a friend of our grandfather's, and it was all shiny brass cogs and wheels and pulleys. We had a drawing of it at home. It was strange to think that our grandfather used to help to wind it, all those years ago, and that he'd stood in that very spot looking across the Mersey and the Wirral and over the Dee to Wales.

'I can see dragons' breath in the Welsh mountains,' Walter said, leaning right out as far as he dared, still not ready to look at Rufus.

'Come on, birdbrain. Get winding.'

All of a sudden Walter wanted to show off. He wanted

to show Rufus that he didn't care anything for what he'd just done to him. 'I'm going right to the top!' he shouted. 'Dare you!'

He heaved himself up the ladder which led to the very top of the tower. It creaked and bent as he climbed it, and he took each step cautiously. Sweat prickled the back of his neck. He could feel the wind rushing round him, cold on his hands and his cheeks, but he daren't climb back down. When he reached the narrow wooden platform that circled the outside of the tower he squeezed himself on to it, his eyes shut tight, his back pressed against the wall, his arms spread out wide to steady himself.

'I'm not an old crow now. I'm an eagle.'

Suddenly the clock machinery started rumbling and the five great bells struck out for the six o'clock, nearly deafening him. He fell sideways and just grabbed the casing in time, or he would have been out, spreadeagled into the air like a great red bird.

He slid back down the ladder and clattered down all the spiral steps without stopping, tumbling out into the well of the belfry on his hands and knees. Mr Thorn scowled at him and jerked his head towards the choir stalls. Rufus was already in his place in the altos, serene in his white surplice. Walter squeezed down the line of trebles on the opposite side, his breath still puffing from him. Ronny, the boy behind him, kindly lifted a cobweb out of his hair.

He had forgotten all about his solo. At least he hadn't had time to feel nervous about it. His heart was still up there, soaring across the sky. And there was I, sitting between Ma and Pa at the back of the church, shaking with worry for him.

When the time for the anthem came and Mr Thorn nodded, Walter's voice seemed to come from nowhere, pure and clear and sweet, and not a second of hesitation in it. Across the stalls Harry winked at him.

'Crow,' Rufus mouthed.

But Rufus had his revenge, you can be sure of that. He set a puma on to us.

Dorothy

Yellow Eyes Menacing

'*Skylark,*' Ma said later, outside the church.

'When I was a boy I could sing like that,' Pa said unexpectedly. It was the first time he had ever mentioned his childhood. It was as if he had never had one, but had always been dignified and stern and dressed in butler clothes since the day he was born. 'Make the most of it, Walter. In no time at all you'll have lost that voice. Know that, don't you? Like a snowflake, a choirboy's voice. Melts away as if it had never been. Pity. Pity.'

He strode ahead of us to wait for the gentry, not swinging his silver-topped cane as he usually did but tapping it on the back of his leg as he walked, like a ticking clock.

Old Salty ambled over to us. He had been tidied up for Sunday by his daughter, his coat and whiskers brushed clean of salt-grains. He slipped a little coin into Walter's hand and closed his hand up over it. 'That's for putting sunshine into a rainy day,' he said.

But we were looking for Master George, weren't we? Miss Caroline and Miss Victoria swept down the path with their heads in the air. Miss Victoria kept her eyes staring ahead of her as though the humble people of the Estate were invisible to her. The Dowager was being pushed in her Bath chair by Timothy, and smiled and nodded at no one in particular, waving as if she was Queen Mary herself. Miss Caroline stopped to talk to one of the families, glancing back towards the church all the time as though she was waiting for someone, and at last she was joined by Master George and the Squirrel.

'Hello, Master George,' Walter called out, and Rufus scowled. Master George smiled slightly. 'Hello, Walter, hello, Dorothy.' And that made me flush, to be singled out like that in front of everybody. To everyone else we were always just the twins.

Miss Victoria turned round and looked at him, a long, quiet, cold look that sent the shivers of winter down us both, and he hurried to join her, and we knew that he was in trouble for yesterday. But we also knew that he couldn't have said a word to her about being with Walter, because there was Pa walking beside her carrying her umbrella and her prayer book just as he always did.

Behind the gentry walked the rest of the servants. We knew them all, but I noticed that there was a new tweeny. She looked scared and proud, and she kept tripping up in her long Sunday skirt, clutching at it as if she longed to hoist it up and run for a change. When she saw me watching her face went crimson. And to my great surprise, she smiled at our Harry, and he smiled at her and nodded, and then ran back into church to help sort out the music with Mr Thorn.

'Does Harry know her?' I asked Ma.

'I doubt it,' Ma said. 'She's only just come.'

'Will I have to be a tweeny before I'm a lady's maid?'

'Not if I can help it. They're treated no better than slaves.'

I stared after the tweeny. I was intrigued by her because of that smile she gave our Harry. I got to know her very well later.

By now it was getting dusky. Walter was still dithery and pleased about his solo and all the praise he was getting. He wasn't keen to go home yet at all, and he asked Ma if he could wait behind for Harry. I decided to wait too, even though some of the boys were hanging round. I tugged on Ma's sleeve to ask her permission, but she was deep in conversation with the coachman's wife and didn't seem to care for the moment what I did. I stayed by the gate where I couldn't be seen by the boys. I could hear Rufus McCartney barking away at them.

'Have you heard about the puma, Walter Hollins?'

'What's a puma?' asked Moses. He didn't go to our church because he was Jewish, but he always hung round after the services to meet the others in case they could play out for a bit.

Rufus sighed. 'It's a huge big cat, as big as you, with great big teeth and claws as long as your fingers. They'd rip you to shreds if he just touched you like that.'

He put out his hand and Moses jumped away from him, half-laughing, half-scared out of his wits.

'And he's escaped from the zoo in town. They reckon he's heading this way. Lots of trees round here for him to hide in. I wouldn't be you for anything, Walter. He's probably hiding in your woods right now. Waiting for you.'

With that he and Bobby peeled away from them and ran off, roaring and leaping on each other as they went.

Moses stared at Walter. 'Shall we walk home together?' he asked. 'Then you could run on after we get to our shop.'

'No, you'll be all right,' said Walter. 'Run on, quick. I'll be with our Harry. You'd better get off now, while it's safe.'

And then all of a sudden I realized that Walter had gone too. He must have changed his mind and charged off after the others while he had the chance. And I was alone in the gathering darkness.

Silence. I looked round, nervous, waiting for Harry to come out. I thought about all the bones lying under the mossy slabs in the churchyard. I couldn't help it. The rooks were flapping down for the night to their high nests in the trees. I wished their croaks weren't so echoey and cruel.

The lights went off in the church and I took a deep breath and ran up the church path. Mr Thorn was standing with his back to me, locking the door.

'Where's Harry?' I shouted, making him jump.

'Harry? Tell your mother he went out by the vestry door, half an hour ago.' He fished his bike out of the hedge and cycled off, whistling Walter's anthem tune.

I ran down to the lane, my hat in my hand. The gas lamps were lit now. They cast a pool of dim light around themselves, with wells of darkness in between. I ran from pool to pool until the lights stopped altogether. Only ten minutes from home, I told myself, toast and jam supper by the fire, and bed. Everything would be all right then. I plunged into the swirly darkness. On one side of me was the tall hedge of a farm field, and on the other the wall of the Holts' estate. I could hear my breath coming out in little flat puffs. I heard a rustle on the field side of the hedge and started to run. The rustle was running alongside, keeping pace with me. I could hear something panting.

'Not scared,' I said out loud. 'Not scared, me.' My voice was such a quaking little thing that it didn't sound like me at all. My heart was bumping about in my chest, de-dum, de-dum. I stopped, and the thing on the other side of the hedge stopped too. I forced myself to run again and just as I came level with the field gate something came looming towards me from the other side. Out of the corner of my eye I saw flicking ears and a long white face. I couldn't stop running. I reached the walls of the Estate and charged round to the servants' gate. Something was walking towards me.

'Dorothy?' It was Walter, come to rescue me as if he was young Will Tanner from one of his stories. 'Ma sent me out to look for you,' he said. 'Where've you been?'

'I heard the puma. On the Holts' estate.' I could hardly get the words out.

'There's no puma. That's just stupid Rufus McCartney trying to scare us. He made it up, Daw.'

'But I heard it!'

I dithered by the wall, not knowing whether to run or walk or stay there all night. An owl shrieked, and we both jumped. I clutched Walter's arm.

'Run for it,' he said. 'It won't go for two of us.'

We ran up to the servants' gate and forced it open, and as I turned round to close it Walter heard what I'd heard, and we both froze. It was a rustle, very close. We left the gate swinging and dived through the clumps of rhododendron bushes. I could see yellow eyes menacing through the branches. I could hear the cracking of twigs and the scrunching of leaves, and feet pounding behind us.

At last we reached the cottage and flung ourselves in, both of us babbling. Ma slammed the door shut and then stood with her back to it. She could see that we were much too frightened to be told off.

'There's no puma. Come and get warm, both of you. It's all right.' She went over to the fire to make us a hot drink.

'But we saw it!' Walter said.

'What about Pa when he comes home tonight?' I moaned. 'He'll get eaten by the puma.'

'There's no puma,' Ma insisted.

'There is. Rufus said it's in all the papers. He said it was heading this way and I saw it. And then Walter did.'

Ma did a very brave thing then. She picked up the metal tray and the poker and opened the door about a foot, and beat the tray like a soldier on parade. Then she stepped back in quickly and slammed the door shut.

'There,' she said. 'That'll do it.'

Harry sauntered downstairs, his eyes red from reading by candlelight. 'What's going on?'

'Oh, they're full of silly talk of a puma, of all things,' said Ma. 'Did you ever hear anything so daft?'

'Oh aye, I forgot about the puma.' He laughed, his hands in his pockets, bigger than his boots and not scared of anything. 'A bit of banging won't do any good. I know how to deal with pumas.' And before Ma could do anything to stop him he was out of the door. We ran to the window, but it was too dark now to see anything. He was away for ages, and we couldn't think of a thing until he was safe home again. Just when we felt we couldn't bear it any longer he came back in, wiping his hands on his breeches and grinning. He winked at us, full of mystery. 'That's finished him off.'

'Now get your supper, and let that be an end to it.' Ma set some warm griddle cakes in front of us, and creamy white butter and raspberry jam, and she sat watching us eat and humming to herself while she darned stockings for next day. We were glad to get to bed that night, but still neither of us could sleep. We were still awake and wondering when Pa came home, much later, about midnight.

'Is it true about that escaped puma?' we heard Ma say, and we both sat up, straining to listen. We could hear the clatter of cutlery as Ma set the table for breakfast. Would he never speak? He would be peeling off his gloves and hanging up his long-tailed coat, loosening his stiff collar.

He scraped back his chair on the flagged floor to sit down. Ma would be helping him off with his shoes.

'There was a puma,' he said at last. 'But not any more. It was shot yesterday down by the Pierhead.'

'Yesterday!' Walter said out loud.

'Poor thing,' Ma said downstairs, and Pa grunted agreement.

We lay back in our bed. On the other side of the curtain Harry snored smugly in his sleep.

'I'll never clean Harry's boots again,' Walter vowed. 'Never. That's that.'

But I was thinking about the pounding feet behind the wall, and the yellow eyes gleaming at me through the shrubs.

We did hear the truth of it, much later, but not from Harry. Oh no. It was Tweeny who told us.

Oh La! Shadders Everywhere!

Puma, my foot!

I knew all about the puma. It was the first thing I heard about when I walked off the ferry from Birkenhead, and I thought, if this is what Liverpool's like, I might as well go straight back home.

Oh, but I wouldn't do that. Not for all the tea in China. I've said goodbye to all that. No, I'm not sorry I come to be a tweeny. Wasn't hard, really, leaving home. Didn't hurt. I was pushed out, mind you. Me mum woke me up one day with a clean frock for me in one hand and a pair of boots in the other and said, 'Gerrup. You're leaving today.'

First I knew of it!

She brought me down to the ferry with two of our little ones and said, 'Do your best for us, girl.' That was all she said. I looked right across the brown Mersey to Liverpool and I thought I'd rather die than cross that water. I couldn't hardly speak, I was that flipperty with nerves. Worst thing was going to be walking down that heaving gangway to the ferry boat. I could see the water chopping up between the planks, and it was all mucky and nippy. Our Billy was tugging at me sleeve and his face was shiny red with crying. And there was Titch, reaching out to me. Oh, little Titch! Except Mum had another one coming, didn't she, so he wouldn't be Titch for long. Number twelve, next one'll be. I hugged him tight, and he put his sticky little fists round me neck and started bawling again, and that set me and Billy off.

No, it doesn't do to think about Titch. What's going to happen to him, now I've gone? My Auntie Lil said she'd have him while Mum's confined, but her house is a rat-hole and no mistake, not much better than ours. It's hell in our house, and I'm telling you the truth. Mum and Dad always brawling and arguing, always a kid crying, and me, being oldest girl, always up to me neck in jobs to do.

Anyway, me luck come when they needed the space on the mattress for the next child, and out I went. I'm to send me money home and I've got the address writ on a scrap of paper in me gloves, seeing as I'm not too good at doing writing. Well, when you're the oldest girl there's no point sending yer to school, is there? Far more use at home. And now, far more use earning money for me Mum and Dad to spend on liquor. Not likely. If they get anything from me at all it'll be breeches and boots for our little kids.

Then the deckhands was shouting at me to get on board quick and I put our Titch down and squeezed Billy till he burped out loud, and I grabbed me bag and ran. 'Ta-ra, Mary!' Billy shouted.

Last time anyone called me Mary, that was. I'm Tweeny now, if you please.

Oh, but Liverpool! What a huge, grand city! I got off the ferry with all the other passengers and they all seemed to know where they was going, didn't they, all running about like spiders to catch trams and cabs, and I just sat there holding me hat on in case the wind blew it away. A lad went past on a bicycle and he winked at me and I thought, oh la! What's to do now? He kept cycling up and down between offices looking important and then he come up to me and said, 'I wouldn't hang about if I were you, there's a puma on the loose.'

'Oh,' I said. 'What's one of them?'

'Look out!' There was a copper running towards us with eyes gobbing out of his head and shrieking away at his whistle as if he was one of them steam trains, and then there's a half a dozen more of them all shimmeying about and shouting, and a great huge car pulls up if you please, so I know it's something what doesn't happen every day and that this puma thing was giving them all a bit of fun and malarky.

No, I didn't see it meself. Wish I had though. They say it was lovely. People round me were saying it was a living animal what escaped from its cage in the zoo and ran wild round Liverpool, and when I heard that me heart kind of opened up and give a little cheer for the puma. Get away! Get away! But then they shot it. Oh yes, I heard the bang. I know they shot it.

Then, blow me, this lad comes back again! He asks me if I'm all right and not too frightened about the puma. He reminded me a bit of me big brother what sailed off to America and never come back. And I took me chance and said in me best voice, 'I'm looking for a job. Is there anything going round here?'

He just laughed. Nice laugh. 'They don't employ young ladies in the offices,' he said, and I went hot and smiley, soft me, because although I'm nearly thirteen nobody's ever called me a young lady before. But then he seemed to take me in, because look at me, there I was in a frock what's just come from the pawn shop and a bag the size of a bonnet to hold all me belongings in. Anyone could see I was desperate.

'They might be wanting someone on our Estate,' he said. 'Wiley said they were short on kitchen staff.'

Me pulse was going ding-dong, ding-dong, but I didn't lower me eyes and I didn't let him see how tight me fists was tucked inside me shawl. Oh, let me, let me, I was saying to meself. A job in a Big House! It would give us a bed to sleep in, and good grub every day. So he pointed out the road I was to take and said if I walked it quick I'd be there in about an hour.

'Look for the big white house,' he said. 'All the others are red sandstone, but the white one's the best. That's where Pa works. Go round the back to the kitchens and ask for Mrs Bains. And tell her Harry Hollins sent you.'

Believe me, I could have pulled him off his bike and hugged him! Lucky for him someone whistled him to get back to work.

'Let me know how you get on,' he shouted, and he

cycled away, whistling. I set off, chanting the names of the roads I was to ask for in me head, and at the end of them, Bark Hill, and Mrs Bains. And there it was, at the end of that long drive, just as he said it was, a huge big white mansion surrounded by trees, and all its windows flashing like pools of rainwater. Oh, me heart was in me mouth when I saw it. Oh please, God, please, God, I kept whispering. Me! I'm going to live there!

Yes, that's how I got me job.

'We need a tweeny,' said Mrs Bains, and her starchy clothes all creaked as she bent down to look at me. 'And you look as if you know what hard work is.'

'I do that, miss,' I told her.

'We'll give you a trial.'

Tweeny. That's me now. I'm in between upstairs and downstairs. I have to help nice fat Joan downstairs in the kitchens, and I also have to help the sniffy parlour maid, Annie, to keep things smart upstairs, polish the doors, polish the stair rails, keep the fires going – and there's over a dozen of them. Keep out the way of the gentry, that's the first rule. Oh, I'm kept busy all right, but I'm used to that, aren't I?

I haven't got no bedroom, but I don't care. I've got a warm shelf to sleep on in the kitchen so I can keep the fire banked all night and get it going before things start in the morning.

First night, I was wide awake, watching the coals shifting about and all them little flames licking and they reminded me of cats, full and sleepy and contented.

I'd just gone off to sleep when I heard this queer noise: creak, creak, creak. Scared, me! But I can't just lie and imagine, can you? I had to find out what was doing it. I'm like that. So I picked up me candle, and crept out the kitchen and into the passage. Oh la, shadders everywhere! There was a door leading down to the cellars, and that's where that creaking had come from. I pushed it open and went down. I never knew how brave I was till that minute. And I saw it, rocking backwards and forwards, backwards and forwards.

So that was me first night in the Big House. Next day I was run off me feet, up and down them stairs all day long, till I didn't know whether I was coming or going, or whether I was supposed to be rubbing the stairs with a dust-cloth for Annie or rolling out pastry for Joan, or what. Just when I thought me legs was going to give up, Bains come down all starch and jangle and told us to get ready for church. Church, me! Oh, it was lovely, walking across the brown fields with the birds flicking about over our heads and the sound of bells just going wild. They knew how I felt. They was singing for me!

And in that huge big red church I thanked God, I did, and that's a thing I've never even thought of doing before. I couldn't take me eyes off them lovely coloured windows, and when that boy sang all on his own it made me shiver. It did. Soft, me! I was busting, trying to keep the grin off me face. When we went out I just clipped sight of the boy on the bicycle, Harry wotsis-name, and we nodded to each other, polite like. But I was flying, me! I wanted to run up and thank him for what he'd done for me.

So after we got back to the Big House and Joan was putting her feet up for five minutes before we started the bread-making, I thought, I'll just nip down the drive and I might catch him coming home from church, and thank him proper. I took a candle and held me hand round it to stop the flame getting blown out, and would you believe it, I got lost. Them grounds look so different in the dark! I traipsed round for goodness knows how long and I kept tripping over roots and leaf piles and bumping into trees. Then I heard these voices. Two children, it was. I started to run towards them holding up me candle so they'd see me. But as soon as they heard me coming they started running and shrieking as if I was the flippin' devil, and they dashed into a cottage and slammed the door behind them.

Now what? I was just finding my way back to the drive when someone started banging a metal tray or something and I thought I was going to die of fright! What a shindig! I dropped me candle and there I was, in the dark and still lost. Well, I thought, I can't be that far from the Big House, but with all them trees in the way there just wasn't a sign of it. The only thing I could do was to go and knock at the door of that cottage and ask them to lend me a light. That was when Harry wotsit come out. He stood with his hands in his pockets whistling and I thought to meself, oh la, I know that tune, here's your luck come back. I went and tapped him on the arm and his bones nearly jumped out his skin.

Anyway, he took me back home safe and Joan cleaned me up and give me a hot drink and then – I can't tell you for feeling choked, soft me – she kissed me goodnight.

Dorothy

A Face at the Window

*W*alter and I had just about got over the puma fright when we had another one. This happened about a week later and it just about spoilt the best night we'd ever had. The gentry were spending the evening with the Holts, and Pa had three whole hours to spend with us. I can't remember that ever happening before. It was wonderful and we all wanted to make it special.

Pa put one of his records on and wound up the gramophone. This time we enjoyed listening to it and he actually let us sing. It was an opera called *The Mikado* and Ma knew every word of it. Did I ever tell you what a beautiful voice Ma had?

'For – he's going to marry Yum Yum!' she sang.

'Yum Yum!' we all chorused, even Pa.

'You'll find there are many who'd wed for a penny, who'd wed for a penny, there's lots of good fish in the sea, there's lots of good fish in the sea!'

We loved that bit. Harry was kneeling on the hearth toasting crumpets on a long fork, and I was buttering them and Walter was spreading them with lovely red sticky jam, and we were singing our heads off all the time.

There was a sad little song about the sun and the moon. Ma stood in the middle of the room with her hand on Pa's chair back singing it to us and we had all gone quiet and still, listening to it by the firelight, and Pa with his eyes closed and a peaceful smile on his face. And suddenly Ma stopped singing. The record played on, but Ma was standing with her hand to her mouth.

'What's that?' she said.

Pa opened his eyes. 'What?'

'I thought I saw a face at the window. Someone looking in at us. There – look.'

'There is someone!' Harry dropped the toasting fork with a clatter and ran to open the door. 'Who's there?' he shouted.

Pa struggled to put his tail-coat on and followed Harry out. 'What do you want? Come out and show yourself!'

We all crowded over the threshold. The opera was still singing away to itself. Pa picked up the broom from the porch and went right round the cottage, poking the bushes with it, but he didn't find anyone.

And I looked sideways at Walter, and he looked sideways at me, and then Ma ushered us all in and made Pa bolt the door and pull the curtains to. It had been a lovely night until then. Somehow Ma didn't have the heart to carry on singing again, and soon Pa had to go back to the Big House to let in the gentry when they came back home from the Holts'. Ma bolted the door after him and packed us off to bed, and not even then did Walter and I talk about it. We didn't need to. We both felt exactly the same. And we both had a snuggly warmth about the evening we'd had with Pa that we didn't want to spoil by talking. It had been one of our best ever, in spite of the peeping Tom. If only we could have Pa to ourselves more often.

And after all that, I went and did something to Pa that was really awful. Now I don't know how I could have done it, and I'm ashamed. But before it happened there was some *very important* Big House news to think about.

A few days after the face at the window, Wiley came to visit Ma with the latest gossip. Ma was out, and when Walter and I arrived home from school there were some twigs on the doorstep arranged in the letter W to show that she had been. Good, we thought. We'll get something nice for tea if she comes back. No sooner had Ma arrived back home than Wiley was there again, bristling with news. We sat on the stairs with a plate of scones between us, pretending to be too busy eating to listen to her. I don't think she knew we were there, she was so keen to tell her story.

'There's such agitation at the House,' she said, perching on the edge of Pa's chair as if at any moment a bell would be rung and she would have to scurry off to one of her tasks. 'It's bad enough at the best of times, but now the whole thing's been exacerbated. The Master's coming home, and then they say he's going to Australia! That ship of his is being launched at the end of the month, and he's going on it! They say – ' And here she lowered her voice and we stopped eating scones so we could hear what she said – 'that he has fallen in love with a lady from Australia!'

She put down her cup and saucer and folded her hands on her lap, nodding away at Ma. 'They say Australia is ten thousand miles away! He's holding a farewell party next weekend so we'll be up to our eyes in work. And the sisters will be in charge of the House until he comes back. *If he comes back.* I daresay they'll be making Herculean endeavours to find husbands for themselves now.'

This was too much for us. We'd been holding our breath too long, I think. We both snorted into our cups of tea, and Wiley realized at last that we'd been listening. She turned her neck stiffly to stare at us. 'Do you always indulge in such impropriety?'

'They both have bad coughs,' said Ma mildly. But as soon as Wiley turned her glance away she glared at us and indicated with a jerk of her head that we were to go outside. We rolled about on the grass howling with released laughter.

'I'm exacerbated,' Walter said at last. 'The Wicked Sister wants to marry Hercules!'

'Stop being impropriotous,' I said, and we howled again.

Ma tapped on the window, and we ran off to climb the tree.

'Australia!' I said, staring out at the river. 'It must be even further than China.'

'That's where Pa's canary comes from, Australia,' Walter said.

I couldn't believe it. I tried to imagine that little yellow bird flying ten thousand miles just to be put in a cage in Pa's pantry. It didn't seem fair. I liked to watch the birds in the air, being busy and quick and full of things to do. From where I was sitting I could see the lapwings beating across the fields with their paddly wings, and all round us big clumsy rooks settling themselves for the night on their untidy nests. We'd be called in soon, when Wiley went back to the House.

'Make up a story, Walter,' I said.

'What about?'

'The face at the window!'

He sat and thought for a minute with his eyes closed. I was watching a family of red squirrels flowing along the branches below. Their tails reminded me of dandelion clocks. Then Walter started to speak, and I forgot all about the squirrels. I closed my eyes and I was in another world. How I love stories!

'A long time ago,' he said, 'there was a man who was the lord of the Big House and all the lands around it for as far as he could see. All he needed for his happiness to be complete was a young bride. One day when he was riding up the drive on his horse, Black Night, an owl flew across. The horse was startled, reared up, flung the man from his back, and trampled on him. He died instantly. But when day came, his body had disappeared and was never found. All that remained was a pool of blood.'

'Horrible,' I said.

'Ah, but his ghost came back to haunt the house that

should have been his. He peered through the window on dark nights when he couldn't be seen. He flung his black cape around himself and tiptoed from tree to tree, lurking in the shadows, searching for the girl who would have been his bride. He gazed at the people inside the House, each new generation, as they came. He looked out for the bride of his dreams. He knew that one day he would find her. He would draw her down into his dead world, and they would live there for ever.'

'Don't!' I said. Shivers were clambering up my spine like icy ants. I had an idea what might be coming next.

'And when he had grown tired of peering through the windows of the Big House, he crept through the shadows to the servants' cottages. Could she be there? He stepped quietly, and if anyone heard a twig crack they thought it was a rat or a field mouse. He came to the lodge cottage and peered in . . .'

'No!'

'And there was the young Dorothea, sitting with her mother and father and her brothers, Harold and the young Will Tanner. "I have found her," the ghost lord whispered, and his breath misted the glass of the window, yet his piercing eyes gleamed through . . .'

I nearly jumped out of my skin when the branch I was sitting on started shaking, and the leaves rustled like furtive footsteps. I was sure the ghost of the dead lord was climbing the tree to get me. Master George's head came through the leaves, red and puffing with effort, and he heaved himself up beside us, sitting astride the branch as if he was riding a horse. He was very surprised to see me there.

'Pretty good effort,' he said, when he'd got his breath back, but I didn't know whether he was complimenting himself or me for getting up there, or praising Walter for his story. 'Came to tell Walter the news. I've had a letter from my father.'

He pulled a crumpled sheet out of his pocket. It looked as if it had been read many times. 'He's down in Tilbury, and he's coming home next weekend for the launching of his new ship. It's called the *Liverpool Lady*, and it will be the finest vessel on the sea!' He lowered his voice. 'Isn't it exciting?'

'I suppose so,' I said. I liked the tall ships best, with their beautiful sails like wings. I thought the steamships were too noisy and bulky. They reminded me of bulls.

Master George folded up the letter and put it in his pocket. 'Father says he has something else to tell me, but it will have to wait until he comes home because he doesn't want to trust such important news to the mail. I think it might be that he's staying home for good. Oh, I hope it is!'

But that wasn't what Wiley had said. Walter and I looked at each other. I tried to remember what she'd been talking about before she'd mentioned Hercules. Hadn't she said something about the Master going to Australia with his boat? I decided to keep my mouth shut and Walter obviously thought the same. He started doing that nervous little whistle of his.

'Wish we weren't having a party,' said George. 'I always have to stay up in the schoolroom and work.'

'The Squirrel is definitely not invited,' I said. 'Your sisters are looking for husbands and Wiley said his attentions are undesirable and unrequited.'

'There'll be flowers all over the place. I hate flowers in the house. They make me sneeze.'

'I hope Miss Caroline marries someone brave and handsome,' I said.

Walter looked up from his scribbling. I don't know how he can write stories and listen to conversations at the same time.

'The suitors will have to perform three impossible tasks,' he said. 'First, kill Aigburth the giant.'

'Aigburth!' I giggled. That was the name of the next village.

'Next, carry a mountain from Wales and put it in the garden here, and third . . .'

'Make Victoria smile,' Master George suggested. 'That would be the hardest one of all.'

He was good fun, Master George, especially that day. He kept bringing his letter out of his pocket and reading it to us again. And I kept thinking, I hope Wiley's wrong about his father. But she never is. Ma says she's better than a newspaper. But we couldn't have told Master George, could we?

Master George

Will I Never See You Again?

I couldn't work at all the day my father was due home. In the past year I have hardly seen him at all because he has been on business in London and Portsmouth. I keep all his letters in the wooden trunk in my room. They nearly make up for not seeing him, but not quite. 'Things are going to be very different,' he wrote in the last one, 'and all will be revealed on my return home.'

I keep wondering what this difference could be. He could have decided to send me away to school, I suppose. I know Victoria wants that. She says it will make a man of me. I don't feel old enough to be made a man of. I'm only eleven, after all. Anyway, she seems to think I am rather a nuisance and she'd quite like me to be out of the way. But Caroline says she cannot bear the thought of my going, which is very strange, because she never has a word to say to me anyway. I rather think it's the Squirrel she wants to keep in the house, not me, though she always says she can't bear the sight of him. The reason why I think this is because when he is reading to us at lunchtimes she is the only one who listens.

I don't know whether I want to go away to school or not. I suppose it would be quite good fun to be with other boys for a change, though now I have Walter and Dorothy to play with things aren't quite so bad. I would rather like to go to their school in the village, but I know Victoria would never permit that.

But the best thing would be if my father were to tell me that he has decided to stay at home now, instead of wandering around the country in the way he has done since Mama died. I lost them both, that dreadful day. I think he cannot bear to be in the House for more than a day or two at a time without her. But I am here, Father! But now at last his dream has come true, and the ship that he has made his passion is to be launched. All the consultations with designers and engineers and accountants are over and done with, and now he can settle down here and dream up some new venture. This is what I hope for most, in my heart of hearts.

I am truly excited at the thought of it. I know the Squirrel thought me a hopeless case today, for I kept craning my head to look out of the window to see if Father's carriage was coming up the drive. Lawrence the coachman set off to meet him hours ago. Please Father, I kept saying, please come soon and save me from any more Latin verbs.

And at last I heard him. With a sigh of relief that must have echoed my own, my tutor closed his book and put away his pens in their walnut box. I heard my father's voice in the hall, and I heard Hollins answering him, and then, great joy! I heard his steps on the stairs and he actually came into the schoolroom. I almost knocked over my table with its dangerous inkstand in my eagerness to reach him. He threw up his hands to register how much I had grown since he had last seen me and then shook hands with me. I responded awkwardly. I had wanted to fling my arms about him, but now I saw that I was considered too old for such endearments.

It seemed that Father and the Squirrel must talk for ever about my latest endeavours in mathematics and the sciences, and then the Squirrel dismissed himself with a slight bow, which I thought was rather smirky, and I was left alone with my dear father. Again he sized me up and down, and made me turn around to see how straight I held myself, and I was pleased that the dreaded rod that Victoria makes me wear every afternoon appears to be having some effect.

'Shall we walk outside, George?' he asked me. 'I have many things to tell you.'

My heart began its slow beat of anticipation. 'Please tell me you intend to stay with me now,' I wanted to beg him, but dared not in case the answer was no.

As we went downstairs together there was much beaming and nodding among the servants who were preparing the house for this wretched party, and who would usually have melted into the woodwork rather than be seen by us. To tell you the truth, I don't usually notice them at all, but Father has a way of being very pleasant to them which I have decided I will try to copy when I become master here. Hollins, of course, always has the same look of polite interest on his face, as if every word my father speaks to him is of extreme importance. I have noticed that Walter has the same air about him.

Even the tweeny was still on the stairs polishing, but Bains coughed and twitched her keys and the poor girl nearly fell downstairs in her eagerness to get out of our way through the door to below stairs, and left her dusting cloth behind her. Bains stepped on it neatly, hiding it under her long skirt.

And when we went outside, the lawns had never looked greener or the trees more majestic. Father stood on the steps with his hands behind his back and took it all in, breathing slowly. I did the same. Everything we could see belonged to us.

'Ah, George,' said my father at last. 'I shall miss all this.'

And my heart drifted right away from me and I understood what it was that he had to tell me.

'Where are you going, Father?' I tried to keep the betraying quake from my voice.

He descended the steps and I followed him. There was a frost in the air, and I remember the smoke from his lips and how it hung about him.

'At the end of the month our glorious ship sets sail for Australia, George. Think of that! This has been my dream for the past dozen years and now it has come to fruition. The greatest ship to sail from the docks of Liverpool, from the docks of England! The *Liverpool Lady*! Now we can establish a shipping line that will be greater than Holt's or Cunard's! It will be yours one day.'

I know that. How many times have I read that in his letters to me?

'And when she takes her maiden voyage, I shall be sailing on her.'

I looked away. There was a threat of tears about my eyes that I did not wish my father to see.

'I intend to establish our offices in Sydney, Melbourne, Perth, Brisbane, Adelaide . . . do you know those names, George? Has your tutor taught you well?'

All I could do was to nod. Australia is a vast country, I knew that. It is a continent. It is thousands of miles away. It takes many, many weeks to arrive there.

'And I have more news for you.'

My heart began to lift. Would he take me with him? Was that what he was going to say?

'I have been corresponding with a dear lady whom I met in Tilbury some months ago. She lives in Australia, in Melbourne, and has returned there. It is three years since your dear Mama died.'

Here he laid his hand on my shoulder, and it was almost more than I could bear.

'The lady's name is Alice Greenaway. I find I cannot live without her. When I arrive in Melbourne in my beautiful ship, I intend to ask her to be my wife.'

We walked on, but my head was such a swim of despair that I hardly noticed where we went. I remember we stopped at the conservatory, and that my father was peering in at the foreign plants that Victoria cultivates there. I could see apricots gleaming like tiny golden suns.

I breathed on the glass, misting it, and the suns grew dim.

Hollins was standing holding the main door open for us, knowing in the way that he did that our walk had finished. Just before we went inside Father turned to look at our Estate.

'I will miss this,' he said again. 'And I will miss you.'

Then I knew for sure that I must remain with my sisters.

'Will I never see you again?' I asked him recklessly.

'When the time is right I'll send for you,' he said. 'That is my promise.'

Dorothy

It's a Very Dangerous Thing

*W*hen Master George told us this I could have cried for him, I really could.

'Just imagine,' I said to Walter when we were walking home from school. 'What if it was Pa who was going?'

We both stopped at the same time, full of the same awful thought. Surely the Master would need someone to look after him when he went to Australia? How could he manage on his own?

We started to run, our arms folded across our schoolbags.

'Pa's a gentleman's gentleman,' Walter said. His voice was bouncing as he ran. 'He's the Master's butler, not Miss Victoria's. He wouldn't want to stay with her.'

'But he wouldn't go, would he?'

We stumbled into the cottage where Ma was paring mounds of dropped apples that Nat had given her. She stood with a twist of apple peel curling from her knife, staring at us.

'Now what on earth is all this about?'

'Is Pa going to Australia?' I burst out.

'What gave you that idea?'

'Because the Master is going and Pa's his gentleman . . .'

Ma sighed. Chop, chop, her knife went into the flesh of the apples. 'He has asked Pa, you are quite right. Your father has never worked for anyone else and never wants to.' She tossed the peelings and cores into a bucket. 'But the Master has done something that no other master would do – he has given Pa the choice. Pa could travel with him and be his gentleman out there in that foreign place, or he could stay and be the butler to the Estate here without him. It's a great worry to your father.' She stopped chopping. 'You mustn't pester him about it.'

'He won't go and leave us behind, will he?'

'He loves the Master.'

And that was all Ma would say, and it was more than she had ever said to us about the affairs of the Big House. She sent Walter off to choir practice and asked me to look for blackberries to sweeten the apples. I wandered past the sailing ship tree, but I didn't climb it. I was upset and angry to see Master George's boots dangling up there as if he owned it.

On the night of the Big House party Walter and Harold and I shinned up the tree and hung there watching the carriages and prancing horses making their way up the drive. All the gentry from round about had come, and some were in cars. They parked in front of the Big House and when all the visitors had gone in and Pa had closed the main door, their chauffeurs went to sit with Lawrence who was learning to drive for the House. Harry ran down to stroke the warm bonnets of the cars. He said he even climbed into the seat of one of them, but I don't believe that for a moment.

All the lamps and candles were lit in the Big House, and all the windows glowed and lit up the lawns. We could hear the strains of the dance music from our cottage, and I imagined pretty Miss Caroline in a powder-blue dress swirling round the ballroom with one of the handsome suitors. Harry picked up Pa's chair and started dancing with it, knocking into the table and the door, making polite conversation with the pans and the kettle as he whirled past them. I was nearly weeping with laughter. He fixed his eyes on the chair as if he was in love with it.

'You dance adorably,' he murmured, barging into the stove.

Ma was boiling milk for us and she suddenly pushed the pan to one side and turned round as if she was going to tell Harry off, but instead she pulled Walter towards her and wrapped her arms round him. He was all boots and knees and he only came up to Ma's shoulder, but she was laughing and swaying with her eyes closed and holding him in her arms as if he was the handsome young man of her dreams. He pulled faces at me as he whirled past. When she let go of him he pretended to be dizzy and kept on spinning round, laughing and pleased with himself.

'I used to love to watch the parties when I worked up there,' Ma panted, collapsing on to a stool and mopping her face with her pinafore. 'Imagine the lovely dresses.'

'Imagine Miss Victoria dancing with Hercules,' Walter said. 'Imagine her kissing him!'

Ma chased us upstairs then for being silly. But she brought our hot milk up to us and sat on our bed while we drank it, brushing her hair in the moonlight, humming softly to the faraway music.

It was nearly dawn when Pa arrived back home. He brought with him some of the leftover cakes and meats and salads. That morning there were hard-boiled eggs for breakfast. We hated them like that. We liked our egg yolks all runny and golden. Walter rolled his egg across the table to me, and I rolled it back to him along with my own. We just didn't fancy them. Ma told us both off for wasting good food.

'I'll eat the yellow eyeball bit,' I said. 'But I can't eat the white bit.'

'Neither can I,' Walter said. 'It makes me think I'm chewing Cook's apron.'

'If Pa was here.' Ma said, 'you would not be leaving this table until every scrap of those eggs was eaten. I've never known such ingratitude.' She pulled Walter's plate towards her as if she would finish the rubbery white scraps herself and then stood up, her hands over her mouth. 'Cook's apron! Now you've put me right off it!'

'Pass them over,' Harold told her. 'I'll have a go. Just swallow them down.'

He wolfed the lot and then ran out to get his bike, full of wind.

At school dinnertime that day I felt headachey and sick. 'I bet it's those eggs,' I moaned. 'They've poisoned me.' I sat with my head in my hands while the other children stood up to leave the classroom. Walter hovered next to our desk, anxious, until Moses jerked his sleeve.

'What's up with Dorothy?' he asked.

'Miss Victoria tried to poison the suitors,' Walter explained. 'Only we ate it instead.'

'Are you poisoned too?'

'Definitely.' Walter stumbled backwards and lay with his legs in the air. 'I'll leave you my fishing net, Moses,' he croaked. 'Farewell, old friend.'

Miss Brogan was putting coal on the fire. When she turned round to see me still huddled in my chair she picked up her cane and rapped it across the top of my desk.

'Out you go, Miss Hollins. The fresh air will do you good. You'll be home in twenty minutes.'

I tried to stand up and fell back into my chair. 'Take her home,' Miss Brogan said to Walter.

'I'm feeling a bit floppy myself, Miss Brogan,' Walter said, but the teacher flapped us both out of the classroom and opened up the windows.

It took ages to get home because I had to keep sitting down to rest. I wanted to die, actually. Walter sat anxiously beside me, his hand on my shoulder. By the time we arrived home he was half-carrying me. Ma sent us both to bed, even though Walter protested that he didn't really feel floppy after all.

'Harry ate most of my egg!' he called downstairs, but Ma wasn't listening.

When Pa came home for his half hour he came straight upstairs and stood in the doorway, his thumbs hooked into the pockets of his waistcoat.

'Your mother tells me you're unwell, Twins.'

'Not much, Pa,' said Walter.

'Dorothy?'

I managed to moan something.

'Speak up,' he said.

'She's ever so hot, Pa.'

'Let the girl speak for herself. Dorothy?'

'Hot, Pa,' I whispered.

'Try and get out of bed.'

Walter jumped out of bed instantly, sure now that he would be allowed to run out and play, but I just struggled a bit and then lay back again, exhausted.

'Get back in, Walter,' Pa said.

Sighing, Walter did as he was told and lay on his back with his arms folded. Beside him I lay with my eyes closed against the knife-slice of light that came over the top of the window-cloth. Through the deafening throb of my head I could hear the whistle of birds, and the sound of Pa's feet as he trudged downstairs again.

Pa put on his long jacket and went back up to the Big House to ask permission to send for the Estate doctor. We heard the clatter of Harry's bike against the wall, and then he ran upstairs to see us. Ma called up to him to keep away from us. He stood awkwardly in the doorway, staring at us.

'Have you been poisoned too?' I asked him.

'I don't think so.' He fished in his pockets and brought out some conkers, which he rolled across the floor to our bed. 'I'm sorry about the puma,' he said. 'But I would have really scared it away if it had been there. I wouldn't have let it get you.'

He tiptoed down the stairs and ran out of the house, and soon we could hear him whooping round the garden with Bobby and Moses, who'd come to call for Walter.

'I'm better now,' Walter called down to Ma, and was ignored. Soon I heard Doctor Faldo arriving in his pony and trap. By this time I could hardly speak. I was aware of Ma sitting at one side of the bed dabbing my head with a damp cloth.

'Did everyone get poisoned?' Walter asked, and the doctor turned round and frowned at him as if he had spoken a foreign language.

'Your sister has scarlet fever,' he announced. I heard Ma gasp. 'Let's have a look at you, boy.'

Walter lifted his shirt.

'You may be getting a bit of a rash. Let's have the other one.'

Harry was brought up, protesting, and subjected to the same scrutiny while Ma sat by the bed and stroked my hand.

'They'll all have to go to hospital,' Dr Faldo told Ma. 'It's a very dangerous thing.' Ma clenched her fingers over my hand, but the doctor's words meant nothing at all to me. Through the blur of sounds about me I heard his voice again. 'Clear the room, Mrs Hollins. Fumigate it well, and don't use it for three days after. Very serious, I'm afraid. You may lose the girl.'

Dreams Can Come True

*W*hen my sister Victoria heard that the Hollins children were all in hospital she made me stay in bed for a whole week. The Squirrel sent work into my room for me to do, but never came in himself. He hovered in the doorway from time to time and asked me a few sentences in French or in Latin, and that seemed to satisfy him. I could hear him in the schoolroom next door, pacing up and down and yawning. Once or twice I thought I heard Caroline talking to him in there, but such a lot of whispering and laughing seemed to be going on that I couldn't really be sure who it was. Perhaps he had gone mad with boredom and had started talking to himself, like the Dowager does.

My father was at his ship all day and by the time he returned I was always asleep, though I tried desperately hard to stay awake for him. My food tray was left at my door for me by Timothy or one of the maids. One day when I lifted up the salver there was a copy of *Rob Roy* under it. I've no idea who put it there but it was better than any plate of mutton or salmon. I read some of it to the Dowager, sitting in her doorway because I wasn't allowed to go near her, shouting out the words. And when she slept I just carried on reading and didn't tell her what she had missed. It was far too exciting.

At the end of the week Dr Faldo was called in and assured Victoria that there was definitely no sign of scarlet fever, and that I had escaped it.

'How are the twins?' I asked him.

He rubbed his nose as if he was undecided. 'One home, one not.' And that was as much as I could find out. But I'm afraid I had too much on my mind to brood on that. My father was due to leave for Australia. We spent his last evening with the whole family in the drawing room. Caroline played some piano pieces for him, and she and the Squirrel actually sang a duet, which was just about bearable. But Father was too excited to pay much attention, and I was too sad. Victoria was in consultation with Bains about household matters, already making changes to the way the house was to be run, and the Dowager fell asleep. So the singers entertained each other and didn't seem to mind. But at least Father was there, smiling at me from time to time from his wing chair, his pipe creating a blue haze of smoke around him. At the end of the evening he asked me if I had enjoyed reading Sir Walter Scott.

'Oh, greatly!' I said. 'Did you send it up, Father?'

'Not exactly,' he said. 'But I helped it on its way.'

That was just like Father. He loved to make life mysterious.

The next day, Victoria and I went to the port to

wave him off. We knew that many of the staff had been invited to attend the launch and so there was a holiday air about the House, but my heart was heavy. Caroline was ill with a migraine and said she couldn't bear to go to the quays with us because they would be so noisy and smelly. Father had already gone ahead with Hollins as he had some papers to sign in the office, and I was desperately anxious in case he had to go on board before we had a chance to say goodbye to him. Victoria's face had frozen and she snapped at me several times in the car for sniffing and scolded Lawrence for driving too fast.

'When Father has gone,' she said, 'there'll be no more driving round in cars.'

When we arrived, the quayside was crowded with people. We found Father outside his office, giving instructions to the cabin boy who was to carry his trunk on board. How I longed to change places with that boy.

Father embraced Victoria, who dabbed at her eyes and pretended to be upset. She loves to manage the Estate without him, I know that. She was already scheming changes. And then he held out his hand to me, but I could not contain myself and instead he put his hand on my shoulder and led me away to where he could speak to me in private.

'George, learn from this,' he said to me. 'Dreams can come true. I had a vision: I had a great dream of creating this ship and sailing in her, and now it has come true! Where would we go if we never had dreams! Eh?'

'I don't know, Father,' I said. I didn't understand then what he meant, yet there was something about his excitement that was so thrilling that I felt my heart lifting for him, in spite of myself.

'Listen. I will come back,' he promised. 'And God willing you will have a new mother then. In a year or so, we will all be together.'

This cheered me too. I had been without him for as long as a year before, and somehow I had got through the time and he had always returned. So I was able to smile and shake hands with him, and then he left us both and went on board the majestic ship that was the pride of the port and of our family. You should have heard the cheering of the crowds, the hooting of ships' sirens and the music of the bands! As the ship's hooter blasted and she pulled away at last, there was a great roar from the people such as I've never heard before, and it was all on account of my father and his magnificent dream.

I looked up at Victoria and her eyes were glassy. I realized that even she was moved by this great occasion.

'It seems that for once he was right,' was all she would say.

We rode home in silence. The cheering and music was still ringing in my ears. I thought of my father sailing all that way on the greatest ship in the world to take our family name to Australia. 'In a year or so we will all be together.' That was what he had promised me. And I believed him. Through all the dreadful things that happened in the next twelve months, I believed my father's words.

Even so, there was something new to think about when Victoria and I arrived home. Hollins met us at the door with the news that my sister Caroline and my tutor, the Squirrel, had eloped.

Dorothy

I Died and Came to Life

Harry was sent home from hospital the next day, and Walter after five days, and I was alone in the isolation ward. I didn't know anything about it. I was in a red-hot fever that made me toss and tremble like a leaf in the wind, and there were times when I floated right away from myself into a burning, white fire. I heard sounds around me like the booming of waves; I was drowning in them and there was no strength in me to save myself. I think I died and came to life again during that time. Children did die in the beds on either side of me. I heard the nurses whispering around them, and I wondered whether it would be my turn next. I heard children sobbing and sometimes I sobbed with them, and sometimes there was no sound I could make, but I felt scalding hot tears burning into my cheeks.

Ma came every day, but I didn't know that. She wasn't allowed in. All she could do was to look on the list by the door to see if my number was still there. If it was crossed off the list, she would know that I had truly died. Can you imagine that?

But at last I did begin to get better and then I was pining to see her, and I couldn't understand why she didn't come and take me home. A letter came from Walter and I cried when I saw his smudgy handwriting.

Dear Dorothy,
I miss you. Ma said you should be home by now but the Wicked Sister sent word that you can't be brought home until next month, to make quite sure you're free of germs. She made Harry and me stay indoors for a week. We're not even ill! But Harry didn't want to miss the launching of the Master's ship so he sneaked out of the window and went anyway. Wiley told Ma that Miss Caroline has run away with the Squirrel, but I can't imagine why, can you? And that means there isn't really a job for Wiley any more, because she was her maid, so she's helping the cook with the puddings for Christmas instead. But there is something much more exciting to tell you. Wiley says the horse is rocking again! I hope you come home soon because I miss you and I have to do all the errands.

Your loving twin,

Walter

And then there was a five-page Will Tanner story called 'The Rocking Horse', and it was so exciting that it sent my temperature right up and the nurse made me lie down for the rest of the day.

And when at last I was allowed to put on my own clothes and was told that I could go home that day, I thought I was going to die again with happiness. Ma was waiting outside the ward for me and I rushed to her and buried my face in her arms.

'Ma! I thought I was never going to see you again!'

And she held me tight, so tight that I could hear her heart bumping, and the little swallowing sounds she was making in the back of her throat. She smelt of the cottage, woodsmoke and baking and the apples stored in the loft. We sat on the tram holding hands and I asked her the question that had been burning in my head for weeks.

'Did Pa go to Australia, Ma?'

She squeezed my hand very tight.

'No, duck. We've still got Pa.' And her voice was really husky.

I will never forget that walk up the drive, with the trees bare now for winter and the frost sparkling from them, and the berries of the holly bush bright as blood. There was Walter peering out of the window, waiting for me, banging on the glass, rushing out of the door to meet me. I have never felt happier in my entire life. Pa came hurrying home at five and took me up in his arms like he used to do when I was a baby.

'Pa,' I said, 'I was frightened you might go away.'

He set me down then and looked at me as sternly as if I'd spoken out loud in church, then he took his handkerchief out of the pocket in his tailcoat and blew his nose.

'Forget that,' he said. 'How could I possibly have gone away and left my little chuck sick in hospital?'

He wound up the gramophone and this time there was

a new recording, Christmas songs, that he had bought specially for today.

'Walter will sing,' he announced, in a proud, quiet voice, and Walter coughed a bit and pretended to be bashful, but I think he'd been practising. It was 'Away in a Manger', my very favourite carol.

When Harry came home he looked at me critically. 'You've gone as skinny as a rat,' he said.

'I'll soon fatten her up,' Ma promised. 'What a thing to say.'

'Come and see what I've brought you.' He took me outside. There, strapped across his handlebars, was a Christmas tree. He brought it inside and bedded it into our coal bucket, and the room smelt like a forest.

Pa's half-hour lasted most of the night. When he had to go back to the House I asked if I could walk a little way with him and look at all the frosty stars. Ma made me wrap up warm and said Walter was to go with me, but I was first out of the door while Pa was still putting on his white gloves. I heard a sudden scurrying in the bushes. Walter ran round the cottage and came back shrugging.

'No one there,' he mouthed. 'Must have been a cat.'

But I knew it wasn't, and so did he. We took a lantern and some scissors, and on our way back we cut down some sprigs from the holly tree near the cottage to decorate our Christmas tree with.

'We'll put some on the door too,' Walter said. 'This will keep the evil spirit away.'

While Ma and I were decorating the tree with berries

and ribbons and candles, he wrote another story, curled up by the fire. Every now and again he read out blood-curdling bits to us, and Ma kept feeling my forehead to check that my temperature wasn't going up. Harry was learning a tune on a tin whistle that a friend from work had given him. He made a sweet, piping sound with it, like a sort of lilting birdsong. Even though there was no recognizable tune to what he was playing, we were all enjoying listening to it. I was thinking how far away that dim ward with the crying children seemed – a thousand miles away, a thousand years ago now – when all of a sudden Ma gave a little start and dropped her bundle of ribbons. She ran to the window and pulled the curtains across.

I had seen the face too, peering in at us. I kept quiet. I didn't want to think about who it might be. I didn't want anything to spoil the best day of my life.

Dorothy

Set the Bird Free

The day after I came home I tested my strength by trying to climb the tree. Walter was at school and Ma had gone down to Moses' shop. As far as she knew I was reading in bed. I thought I had lost the knack of climbing at first. I didn't seem to have the strength to pull myself up, but I took it slowly and at last I had made it.

When I reached our branch I put my arms around her trunk and pressed my cheek against her, like I sometimes did to Hercules. My old tree! My sailing ship. Then I heard a whistle below me and looked down to see Master George pulling himself up. I was disappointed. I think I really wanted to be on my own that morning.

'I couldn't wait to see you!' he called out.

I leaned down, suddenly pleased to see him too.

'You didn't get it then?' I asked him.

'I might as well have done. Victoria made me stay in my room for a week, just in case. And when I saw Harry and Walter in church and not you, I was really worried.'

I didn't know where to look, I was so pleased with him.

'Father's gone. You know that, don't you?' he asked.

I had forgotten. I'd been so glad that Pa had stayed

with us that I had quite forgotten about how wretched Master George must be feeling.

'I don't know when I'll see him again,' he said. 'He wants to get married. What if Alice Greenaway doesn't want me as well? He won't want me then, will he?'

I can't tell you how sorry I felt for Master George. I wish now that I had been able to say that to him, but I didn't, you see. I was too shy and then it was too late.

'Everybody else knew for ages that he was going away, but nobody told me. I didn't even have time to get used to it. That was the worst thing. Everyone knew about it except me. Did you know?'

'I think so,' I said.

'Even the servants' children!'

We were both quiet for ages. I was wondering if I should tell Master George that he should be feeling happy because he hadn't caught scarlet fever, and because his father owned the grandest ship in the world, and because he lived in the beautiful Big House and had my Pa as his butler. There were all kinds of reasons for him to be happy. Just sitting up there in the tree made me happy. I was trying to work out how to say all that to him without it sounding cheeky or as if I didn't care, when he muttered something that was so interesting that I asked him to say it again.

'I've got a secret,' he said.

'Tell me then.'

'And you'll never tell a soul?'

'Of course I won't.'

'Not even Walter?'

I was thrilled. I had never been asked to keep anything from Walter before. There wasn't really much point. I wondered how long it would be before he guessed it anyway.

'All right,' said Master George, 'it's this. I wish I was you.'

I wanted to laugh. It was such an odd thing to say. It was so big, and so nothing. What kind of a secret was that supposed to be! 'Me? How could you wish you were me? I'm a girl!'

'Walter then, I wish I was like you or Walter.'

I thought about this. It didn't make any sense to me, that didn't.

'I do. I wish I lived in your little sandstone cottage. I hate living in the Big House. I wish I'd got a mother and that my father lived at home and we all had Sunday tea together and sat listening to music round the fire. It's not fair.'

That was how I knew for sure that it was Master George who'd been peering through the window of our cottage at us. And something about knowing it made me go cold as if there were snowflakes licking my skin. I was cold inside too, hard and cold and wanting to cry. I felt as if he'd stolen something from me. It was our own special time. It was nothing to do with him.

'We don't see Pa much,' I muttered. My face was flaming, I could tell. I wanted to go home.

'Now say you wish you were me.' He had that

commanding, ringing tone to his voice that made me think of Miss Victoria. It made me mad, that did.

'No,' I said. 'I don't wish I was you. I'd hate to be you.'

His face was puffy and sort of folding up round his eyes. I couldn't bear to look at him.

'I wish I hadn't told you now,' he said.

He was crumpling a dead leaf in his hand, twisting it round and round by the stem, spiking his thumb with the pointed twiggy end. I wanted to snatch it away from him.

'You needn't worry. I won't tell anyone, if that's what you're thinking,' I said. But I made my voice sound as mean as possible. 'I can keep your stupid secret.'

'You've got to tell me a secret now. Go on. I told you that. You've got to tell me something like that.'

'I haven't got anything.'

'You must have,' he shouted. 'Go on. Something, Dorothy Hollins. I order you to.'

I wanted to swing back down the tree but I couldn't, he was in the way, straddled across the branch with his back against the trunk as if he was the lord and master of the tree. I wanted to push him off.

'All right,' I said at last. 'I suppose I could tell you about Pa's bird.'

'His bird?'

'He's got a yellow canary in that pantry of his in your house.'

Master George was scornful. 'What if he has? What's so special about that?'

'He keeps it there out of spite.' I don't know what was brewing up in me to make me say that.

'A stupid bird! What good's a stupid bird!'

'He keeps it because he hates being your servant and doing things for you all the time. He keeps his canary in the pantry to remind him that there's a bright sunny day outside, and when he listens to it singing it makes him think of Ma . . .'

Master George had his eyes closed now. It helped me to shout at him. It helped me to hate him. I wanted to make him cry.

'It makes him think of when we're all at home sitting round the fire toasting crumpets and you're in your great big house and it's all cold and quiet and lonely . . .'

'Stop it, Dorothy. Stop it!'

But I couldn't, you see. There was a bad crow inside me, flapping its ugly wings. 'He keeps it out of spite to remind him of that. And then he doesn't mind being your servant.'

'You're making it up,' Master George said.

'No I'm not. He has got a yellow canary.'

There was a long, long silence. It was beginning to spot with rain. I could hear the slow beat of it on the dry leaves under the tree.

'It's cruel to keep birds in cages,' Master George said, very quietly, as if he just had to say something to break the silence between us.

'It's cruel to keep servants in houses.'

'Don't be silly. Servants can go away.'

'Where to?'

I could feel the rain now. It was dripping off the branch right above my head and sliding down the back of my neck. I had to nudge myself nearer to Master George to get away from it. I lost my balance and he caught hold of my arm and steadied me.

'Dorothy, don't let's quarrel,' he said.

'No,' I said. 'I'm sorry.' And I did mean it.

'So am I.'

'Can we do something to show we're both friends?'

'What though?' I did want to be friends with him. I wanted to take it all back, every word of it, but it had been said, hadn't it? And the shouty horrible words were ringing in my ears like the showering rain on the leaves, like a loud, insistent dance.

'Let's set the bird free.'

It was Master George's idea, but I didn't have to do it. I wanted to be friends with him. I wanted to make up to him for everything I'd said, and for his father leaving him behind like that as if he didn't want him any more. So we did it together. We went round to the kitchen quarters and peered through all the little windows until we found Pa's pantry. It was empty and the door through to the kitchen was closed.

I can't believe how easy it all was. The pantry window was open just a little bit and I squeezed in and pushed it open further so Master George could climb through. The fire was dancing away in the grate. We could hear scurrying feet in the kitchen on the other side of the door and Joan's loud voice laughing at something somebody had said.

Master George pulled Pa's chair over to the window and climbed on to it. He opened the door of the cage.

'Come on, little bird, out you come,' he said, and he put his finger inside a bit nervously. The canary fluttered round on its perch and turned its back on him.

'Come on, you silly lemon,' he said, and shook the cage. We both started giggling.

The canary flung itself out of the cage and swept round the pantry. It danced on Master George's head and swept round again. We both ducked, spluttering with suppressed giggles. Then it saw the window and fluttered over to it.

'No, don't let it go,' I said, suddenly realizing how Pa would feel, but it was too late. Out it went, hovered for a second, and then launched itself up into the air. By the time we'd both scrambled out of the window it had gone out of sight.

We both ran off then, Master George to the main entrance of his house and me right up across the lawns to our cottage. My heart was bursting with excitement and misery. I didn't know what to think now. I just wanted to be friends with Master George, you see. I wanted him to like me as much as he liked Walter. He was my friend first, after all. I never thought how much I would hurt Pa by doing it.

But at least no one had seen us.

I See Everything

I saw them.

There's one thing about being a tweeny that I like. I'm invisible. Nobody sees Tweeny. I have to slip upstairs to do me polishing and melt away in the shadders when the gentry come past. I have to take me orders from Mrs Bains or Joan and keep out of everybody's way while I'm doing me jobs. Everybody's busy, nobody's got time to notice me. Set the tray for the Dowager and run up to her maid with it and disappear quick. Collect the scraps for the cats and disappear quick. Rub the doors and floors till I can see meself in them, but don't let nobody see me. Nobody notices me as long as I do me job. I'm everywhere and I'm nowhere. Nobody sees me and I see everybody.

The things I could tell you about this house! I could have told them upstairs about that Squirrel person and Miss Caroline. I used to see them holding hands. I heard them whispering in the rose walk when I went to feed the cats. I knew what they was planning. Oh la, I thought, they're sweethearts, them two! But I kept me mouth shut because it was none of me business.

I knew the Master had spent the family fortune on that

big boat because I heard him telling the Dowager about it when I was polishing the door. She just giggled. He thought he was quite safe telling her because her brains have gone soft.

I know something else. There's nothing soft about the Dowager's brains. She's a clever one, she is. She talks to her dolls as if they was real humans. Great huge conversations she has with them about what's going on in the world, and she's got a different voice for every one of them, and they all say clever things! It's marvellous to hear her. She should be on the stage.

She's got a house in her room that's a model of the Big House, and when she thinks no one's looking she takes all the gentry and servants and furniture outer it and puts them in the wrong places. She puts Miss Caroline's pinanio in the kitchen and lets the maid play it. She lets Cook put her feet up on Miss Victoria's chaise longue. She takes the horses out the stables and puts them in the library. What's soft about that? She's a good laugh, she is.

I could tell you about Miss Victoria too. She's got a broken heart. Everybody hates her and she's got the sharpest tongue in the world. She's a nasty piece of work and no mistake, but that's because of the state of her heart. She's got a letter in her bureau drawer and she takes it out every now and again and reads it, but she doesn't need to look at the words. She says it to herself while she's looking in the mirror or out the window. Not out loud. I can't hear a word of it or I'd tell you, but I can see her lips going. There's something like hair in the envelope too.

I'm not kidding, her heart's been broke in two and I don't suppose it'll ever mend now.

And then there's all them cats of hers – but that's a different story.

And there's Master George. I like him. I don't see much of him though. He's always upstairs with some tutor or other – when the Squirrel left they brought in another one. I call him the Foghorn. I can hear his voice booming up and down the stairs. He won't last long. But I see Master George pacing round with that rod across his back and I think, I'd rather be polishing stairs than doing that, for all your money. I'll tell you something else. As soon as he gets the chance he wriggles out of his coat, sticks the rod in the aspidistra pot and runs down the drive to that tree. He thinks no one sees him! I tell you, I see everything.

Even when that sister of his made him stay in bed in case he'd caught the fever, he had to wear his rod a couple of hours a day, and just sit up there on his own reciting his numbers or something. I did a daft thing that week. Could have lost me job for it, now I think back. Soft me. I had his tray to take up and I was walking past the library with all them books what I have to dust and I thought, I'll give him one to read. So I put me tray down and crept in and just pulled one off the shelf. And suddenly the Master was there behind me and I jumped right out me skin, I'm telling you. He took the book out of me hand and looked at it and laughed out loud.

'Is this for you, Tweeny?'

I went scarlet. The very idea that I would have pinched a book! I picked up me tray so's he could see where I was off to. 'It's for Master George, sir,' I said, as polite and posh as I could.

And he raised his eyebrows and put his head to one side, studying me a bit, and I didn't know where to put meself and that flippin' tray was rattling in me hands like a tinker's cart. 'Well, Master George won't be interested in Greek political theory, though I'm sure he'll be grateful that you intend to edify his mind.'

'Yes, sir.'

He knelt down and picked out another book and opened the pages as if they was china plates, he was that careful. 'This was my favourite story when I was his age.' He lifted up the salver what was keeping the marmalade pudding warm, and popped the book under it.

Thing was, he could have taken it up himself, couldn't he? They're like that, the gentry. There's all kinds of things I could tell you about them.

The rocking horse? Oh yes. I've seen that too.

Oh, there's things I could tell you about this house. I could write a book about it. I could, only I can't write. Can't read neither, so it wouldn't be no good to me, would it? Eh, I'd like to though. Soft me.

Do you want me to go on, Miss Dorothy? I saw you letting that yellow bird go.

Dorothy

But There is a But . . .

When Pa came home at five o'clock his face was as white and stiff as his shirt front. He sat upright in his chair and he didn't say a word to any of us. I thought about yesterday when Ma brought me home from the hospital, and how he'd come almost running up the path to see me and hugged me as if I was a baby again. That was yesterday, and today he was white and silent in his chair and didn't have a word or a smile for any of us. He put on the horrible growly orchestra recording that we all hated. Ma crept round the room on her tiptoes shaking her head at us as if to tell us that she had no idea what was going on. But I knew.

As soon as Pa had gone, Ma let out her breath in a big whoosh and said, 'Something's upset your Pa. I've never seen him quite like this before. I hope it's not bad news about Germany and France. There's such awful things going on in Europe. Heaven help us if there's another war.'

Walter pulled my hand away from the book I was pretending to be reading. 'What's happened?' he whispered.

'How should I know?'

'Because you do, that's all. What's going on?'

There was such a lump of guilt in my chest, like a great stone, that I wanted to tell him there and then. I wondered if the canary would die in the cold. I was longing to ask Walter if he knew. I wondered if it would fly all the way back to the country it came from and be happy in the sunshine there. I wondered if it would rather be in the cage in Pa's nice warm pantry with the fire burning and Pa whistling to him while he counted the silver. And what would Pa do now, without it? I wanted to say all of this to Walter, but I couldn't because I felt so guilty, and because it was all to do with Master George and the secret he had made me keep. I felt so miserable about it that I didn't know what to do with myself. How could I have done that to Pa? Only one thing would have made me better and that would have been to tell Walter. He was staring at me as if it was written all over my face and he was reading it.

When we were having breakfast the next morning, Harry said, 'That's a funny noise! Can you hear it?'

We stopped chewing and listened.

'A funny sort of whistling. There!'

He ran to the door and looked up 'Hey! There's a yellow bird up the tree.'

And sure enough, there it was in the holly tree near to our house. I knew exactly what it was.

'It's a canary!' Ma said. 'What the blazes is a canary doing here?'

'I think it's Pa's,' I said, in a voice that was so tiny with fluttering gladness that only Walter heard me.

'It's Pa's canary!' he shouted. 'Get it down!' And he pranced round the tree with his arms in the air as if he could jump right up and scoop it off the branch. The canary stepped back a bit and warbled.

'Don't, Walter, you'll scare it off,' Ma warned.

We stood round the tree, hopeless. There's no way you can climb a holly tree, not unless you want to get torn to shreds. Ma brought out a saucer of cold porridge and held it up, but the bird took no notice at all. It cocked its head to one side and whistled quite cheerfully, as if to thank us for our efforts.

'We'll have to catch him,' Ma sighed. 'He won't stand a chance out here in this cold.'

Harry wheeled his bike over to the tree. 'I'm going to climb on to the crossbar,' he said. 'Ma and Dorothy, you hold the bike steady. Walter, hang on to my legs.'

He was like the tightrope walker in a circus that Ma's brother took us to once. There should have been drums rolling for him and a ring of people sitting with their mouths wide open with wonder. He climbed up, steady and calm, and stood upright on the crossbar with his arms spread out on either side to steady him. Walter had his arms wrapped round Harry's knees and Ma and I dug our heels into the grass and kept the bike as still as we could. Harry brought his arms slowly in front of him as if he was swimming, and stretched out his fingers. He just touched the canary and up it flew, out of his grasp, and landed on our flat porch roof.

Quick as a flash, Ma let go of the bike and disappeared into the house. I lost my balance, Harry lurched towards the holly bush yelling his head off, and with the strength of ten men Walter hauled him away from it. The three of us landed in a shouting sprawl of arms and legs, not a scratch on any of us. And there was our brave Ma, standing on the porch roof with a flapping paper bag in her hand and a look of pure triumph on her face.

'Got him!' she shouted.

Well, that's how Pa got his canary back. He never knew how it had escaped. Walter knew it was something to do with me, but he never guessed that Master George was in it too, and of course I didn't tell Master George about it. I didn't want him to know how upset Pa had been. We were friends again, that was the main thing.

But all over Christmas I didn't see him at all. They had relatives to stay at the Big House, but they were all stuffy grown-ups. We weren't invited to the servants' hall to receive our Christmas presents that year. It was always Miss Caroline who did that for us, and she was away somewhere being Mrs Squirrel. We saw the gentry at church on Christmas Day as usual, and the Dowager nodded and smiled and waved her hand at us from her Bath chair, and the Wicked Sister kept her face closed up as if it would crack in half if she let it smile. Master George was there, and he didn't smile either, but I knew that it was because he hadn't heard anything yet from his father.

I didn't see him again to talk to till near the end of February. It was a cold, bright day and he and I were sitting together on our branch on the sailing ship tree. We could see for miles and miles over the frosty fields that day. Steam ships and cargo boats were coming and going all the time on the river, and their hoots were like voices from far away, speaking to us over the water.

Walter was playing knights on horseback with Moses and Hercules, and I was as pleased as punch that Master George had chosen to stay with me instead. I could tell as soon as I saw him that something wonderful had happened.

'Look, Dorothy, I've brought something to show you.'

I was wickedly glad that I was there on my own with him, and that Walter was missing it. It was a letter from the Master. It had arrived on yesterday's packet boat. Master George read it to me, and you could tell by the way he kept looking up from it and beaming that he already knew it off by heart.

'My dear son,' he read, 'Adelaide is a fair, pleasant town with the friendliest of people and the strangest of animals. You have heard of kangaroos? Well, I have seen them! They sit up on their hind legs in the most curious fashion, and their dear babies peer at you from their pockets. Off they bound, as if their legs were on springs! And the birds are bigger and brighter than I would have thought possible, and make the most appalling racket! Truly, my son, Australia is an amazing place. I want you to see it for yourself one day, and you will! Be patient! Ah yes, my dear Miss Greenaway has consented to marry me one day. However, there is a but . . . and you shall hear about it before too long.'

There was more in the letter, about the *Liverpool Lady* only taking twelve weeks to make the journey to Perth, instead of four months, and how she would be returning to Liverpool with a cargo of gold. And when she made her next voyage to Australia, she would be carrying two thousand emigrants, all set to make their new lives over there.

'I wish I could go with them,' Master George sighed.

'You will, one day,' I said. 'But wait till you're grown up and married, and I could be your wife's maid and go with you.'

Yes, I would have liked to do that.

It was a long time before I found out where Walter had been that day. He should have been with Harry, but he wasn't. He was with Moses and then Rufus, though he hadn't played with Rufus for a long time, and they did something awful. In a way what he did was exactly the same as my do with the canary, only it turned out much worse. I blame Rufus myself. This time it was Tweeny who got hurt by it. Poor Tweeny. That's how I got to know her. It was all to do with Miss Victoria's cats.

Dorothy

Holy Smoke

This is what Walter told me, much later

Walter and Moses were having rides on Hercules in the paddock when Rufus sauntered up. Master George and I could actually see him from the tree, leaning on the fence and leering at them. I think he was jealous of little Moses.

'Come on, Walter,' he shouted. 'I'm going to have some proper fun.'

'I'm all right here,' Walter said. He'd never had much to do with Rufus since that day up in the church tower when Rufus had banged his head on the bell.

But Moses was interested. 'Where are you going?' he asked.

'Nowhere for little boys.' Rufus started loping off, and Moses slid off Hercules and wriggled his nose the way he does when his spectacles are sticking.

'I want to come,' he said. 'I'm bored of horses.'

'We'll have to stay on our Estate.' Walter said, 'because I've got to chop wood with Harry when he gets home.'

Rufus waited for them to catch up. 'You choose what to do then.' He was pretending to be generous. I know him.

'We could go and look at the cats,' Walter suggested.

As far as Rufus was concerned this was definitely a good idea. The cage was beyond the greenhouses, which were strictly out of bounds, so they'd have a lot of fun dodging Mawks. Walter only knew about it because Master George had taken him there a few times. As they ran through the kitchen gardens they could see Mawks stooping over the parsnips, his face the colour of ripe plums. They had to go through a gate into the courtyard, and when Mawks heard the latch click he straightened up with his hand on one knee and glared round him. The boys ducked down, spluttering into their fists. At last they were through the courtyard and into the field. At the far end a huge wire cat cage was built round a tree. Inside the cage, cats darted up and down the branches – tabbies, black and whites, ginger toms, stripies, skinny alley cats and fat lazy bundles stretching and scratching on the grass.

The boys peered in through the wire mesh, and the cats peered out at them, yowling now for food. There were a couple of bowls of water and some food scraps on the ground, but they were obviously hoping for something better.

'Holy smoke!' said Rufus. 'What a pong!'

A skinny, grey cat poked its paw out of the mesh and latched on to Walter's jumper with its claws.

'Gerroff!' said Walter. He tried to unhook it and got a scratch on his hand for his trouble. That was how I knew. As soon as I saw that scratch, I knew.

Rufus tried the door. 'Hey, it's open,' he said. 'In you go, Moses.'

Moses backed away. 'They'll attack me.' He looked at Walter for support. 'I'll go in if you do.'

'Who's scared of a few cats!' Rufus jeered. 'Come on, we'll all go in.'

All the same, he pushed Moses in front of him. But the cats were more scared than the boys and set up such a terrible yowling that they must have been heard from the Big House. Then one of them launched itself at Moses and peeled the skin off his leg. He gave a yell and ran for the door, with the others piling out after him. They raced across the field and into the courtyard, and then stopped to examine Moses' wound. There was blood all down his leg and all over his boot. As soon as he saw it he turned white. The others whistled in admiration.

'Come on, Moses, old chap,' said Walter. 'Can you walk?' Moses limped a few steps. 'I think I can manage.'

'Can't die from cat scratches, can you?' Walter asked.

'Not usually,' said Rufus. 'Sometimes.'

'We'd better get him home,' said Walter.

Proud of the attention he was getting, Moses limped across to the gate. Every now and then he stooped to examine his leg and gave a little groan, and the others exchanged worried glances. Mawks was sitting in his potting shed. They could see the smoke from his pipe billowing out of the door.

'Run!' yelled Rufus. He hoisted Moses on to his shoulders and charged round the back of the greenhouses and into Hercules' pasture, and that's where we saw them again. Walter ran to our gate just as Harry arrived home. That left Rufus bent over like an old carthorse, and Moses sitting upright on his back, smiling all over his face.

Now the rest of that story really belongs to Tweeny.

I Love Them Cats

I like working here, most the time. I hate being ordered about all day long – do this, do that, carry this, carry that. But then I think of me dad bawling away at us, and all me brothers and sisters crying and shouting and hungry for food all the time and I think, I know where I'm better off. Hang on to this job, girl, or you'll be in the same boat as your mum.

What I do like here is when they make me do the polishing. Them rosewood doors is best. I go into a dream when I'm doing them. I stare right into the colour, and it comes out the dark wood like a fire. And them brass surrounds on the fireplaces – I'm that proud of the way I can make them gleam, but it doesn't half give me gip in me knees. And I just love polishing the stair spindles. Timothy told me there's sixty-two of them altogether, and he's learning me to count them. Oh la! Me, doing counting! But the best job of all is feeding Miss Victoria's cats. I love them cats, I do.

Every day, Joan gives me a bucket of scraps and a bucket of water to carry to the cats. First time she did it, I couldn't believe what she was asking me to do. Feed cats? That's what rats and mice are for.

'They're in a cage, duck,' Joan said, and her pink face went all fluffy like it does sometimes when she's upset. 'Miss Victoria sends Timothy out to look for strays and he has to bung them in that cage of hers. Just for her to go and look at from time to time. And they're breeding like billy-o, you can imagine! I don't think she likes cats at all. I don't think she likes anything, the old sour face!'

She just mouthed that last bit because Bains was around, and when I giggled Bains turned her head sharp and flicked her fingers at me to get on with me work.

So that's what I do once a day, and eh, it's wonderful to get out the House and breathe fresh air, and I don't care if it's bucketing down with rain or if the tide has turned and brought a howling gale with it. I wouldn't miss feeding them cats for nothing on earth.

I was petrified of them at first. First time I went up to the cage they was snarling and spitting at me through the wire, tearing each other and yowling like the very devil. I pulled open the door and tipped the scraps and water in all over them, and then I ran for me life!

I never dare go right in, even now. I just edge me hand inside and grab the bowls and fill them up quick, and then shove them back in. But I like the cats now. I think they like me. I've got names for them all. Honey, Blackie, Starface, Twitch, Stripey Joe, Howling Minnie, Growler, and so on. I say their names to meself as I'm coming over the field to them, and it's like a song. It's my song.

Then one day something worse than a nightmare happened. I went down as usual and I couldn't make out why there was such a hush in the field as I was traipsing across it. Except for the old crows there wasn't a sound coming.

I soon found out. The cage door was open, and the cats had gone. All of them! I dropped me buckets, spilt water all over me boots, and I ran round the field shouting for them – 'Button, Michael, Grey-face, Squidge!' I scrimmied on me hands and knees under the hedge, yelling out all the time for them, 'Twiggy, Hisser, where are you? Please come home, please come home!' And, honest, there was tears running all down me face because I wanted them so bad, even though it wasn't much of a home for them to come back to, was it? I found one of the new kittens, dead. It hadn't even got a name yet. I put it in a bucket and carried it back to the House.

When I showed it to Joan she shouted at me and told me to get rid of it at once. Then Bains come over to find out what all the fuss was about, and I couldn't speak for crying, and she called Timothy to go and tell Hollins to report to Miss Victoria that all her cats had gone.

Next thing, there was an outing to the cage. Timothy, Wiley and Hollins and Master George and Miss Victoria herself – can you just see it! They all put their coats and hats on and went down to the field, and spent half an hour poking under hedges proving to themselves that it was true, that the cats had really gone.

And then, Miss Victoria said she wanted to speak to the person who fed her cats, and I was sent for. It was the first time, ever, that I'd been inside the gentry's drawing room when any of them was there, and if it had been full of wild pumas I wouldn't have been more scared, honest.

Bains took me up to that door what I'd polished so beautiful that very morning, long before anyone in the house got up. She muttered at me to stand straight and speak up and tell the truth. And then she knocked and Hollins opened it up. His face didn't say nothing to me at all. He just nudged his hand a bit to show I was to go in.

'The tweeny,' he announced.

I bobbed, like I was supposed to. There was firelight dancing all round the walls. The edges of the paintings was all glowing with it. What a nice room, I thought. Me favourite. The Dowager was sitting by the fire with a rug across her knees singing a little song to herself. She's got a sweet voice, that old lady has.

'Grandmother, please be quiet,' Miss Victoria snapped. Like a pair of sharp scissors, her voice is. I saw her peeking at me in the shaddery corner, and Hollins nudged me in the back so I had to go right up to her. He carried a lamp across and put it on the table next to her, so she could look at me proper. Her face was all poky and pale.

'So you are the child who feeds my cats?'

I must be stupid, but that was the first time I realized that she was trying to blame me for them cats going off. It had never entered me head before. I stood up straight and clenched me pinny in me fists.

'They was all there when I fed 'em yesterday, Miss.'

'Then why aren't they there now?'

Me brain was spinning like a top. I remembered that latch clicking behind me yesterday, definitely it did. 'I shut the door, Miss. I know I did. I shut it proper, like I always do. Ah, Miss, there's kittens in that cage. I wouldn't want the old owl to be nobblin' 'em, would I?'

Over by the firelight the Dowager perked up. 'I like the kittings best.'

Miss Victoria stood up sudden, with them black skirts of hers rustling round her. She was like a big paper bag.

'You're a careless, lazy, insolent child.'

Eh? Does she mean me, I thought, but I kept me face shut.

'You deserve to be sent away, but Bains has already pleaded on your behalf to let you stay, your mother and your father having so many mouths to feed.'

'Thank you, Miss.' I bobbed again. Crikey, I thought. And there's me calling Bains all the names under the sun! 'The wind must've got the door,' I suggested, trying to be helpful now. 'I should get Timothy to put a bolt on it, Miss.'

'I did not ask for your advice, Tweeny.'

'No, Miss.'

'You may sleep in your bed tonight, but tomorrow you are to be put in the cage and kept there all day and every day until the cats are found.'

The room went so quiet that I thought the old lady and Hollins had both died. I felt like dying meself. Then Miss Victoria flapped her hand at me and I heard Hollins opening the door. I nearly fell out the room. I ran past

Bains and down our stairs to the kitchen, and Joan smothered me up in her fat arms and found me a rag to wipe me eyes with.

'She's a wicked, mad woman,' she said. 'All money and no heart, that's her. Thinks she can treat us like dirt.'

The housekeeper stood clicking her tongue, but Joan wasn't going to be shut up now. 'It's true, Mrs Bains, I'm sorry to say it but it's true. She thinks more of her cats than she does of human beings, and she doesn't treat them right either.'

'I'm glad they escaped,' I said. 'And I didn't leave the door open. I know I didn't.'

I can't tell you how I fretted that night. I lay as stiff as a poker on me shelf by the range and I didn't sleep a wink. I could hear Timothy snoring his face off on his bed outside Hollinsw's pantry, and I could hear rats scuttling out in the yard. The big clock up in the hall donged the hours away. And I tell you something else I heard. The creaking of that rocking horse, that's what I heard.

I was glad when morning come at last and the cockerel started crowing. I could make a bit of noise meself then, poking the fire and riddling the ashes. I went out to the yard and pumped water up. There was ice on the step. I thought, this time tomorrer you'll be dead, Mary Rogerson. You'll have froze to the grass. Timothy come out to the yard, yawning and stretching and scratching himself as if he was one of the missing cats. He stuck his head under the tap and sluiced himself down. He came out of it gasping, shaking himself like a dog.

'Never mind,' he said to me.

I carried the bucket of water into the scullery to wash meself, and the maids started coming down from the attic rooms with crusts of sleep in their eyes. Joan stirred the porridge in the great black pot, and as soon as she shoved the bowls on the table, Bains and Hollins appeared, smart as soldiers. Nobody said nothing.

After breakfast Timothy picked up the rug from me shelf and rolled it under his arm. 'Ready, Tweeny?'

Joan pushed a loaf into the pocket of me pinny, and Bains just stood and watched her.

'The woman's wicked!' Joan said. The tears were streaming down her cheeks. 'Locking a child in a cage!'

I wasn't crying. I felt sick, but I wasn't interested in crying. Past it, I suppose. I felt as if I was going to the hangman. Timothy opened the kitchen door for me as if I was one of the gentry, and I just folded up me mouth and followed him to that cage.

Dorothy

That's a Cat Scratch, Walter Hollins

'There were six wild pumas in the jungle pit.' Walter read. Harry snorted and put his jacket on to go out. As he opened the door we could hear the cold howl of the wind across the lawns.

'Snarling and roaring and rolling about,' Walter went on. 'The boy prince lay among them, gashed from head to foot. He was bleeding to death. "Save me!" he gasped. Young Will Tanner stood, brave and defiant, at the entrance to the pit. He drew his sword with a flash, and the huge puma leader turned from the prince and eyed Will. It crouched low, ready to pounce . . .'

'My goodness, Walter,' said Ma. 'You'll frighten your sister to death one of these days.'

'Go on, Walter,' I said.

'Put some more coal on the fire first,' Ma said. 'Pa will be here any minute.'

I tipped the bucket of coal on to the grate. The coals were damp, and they hissed through the bars. The long tongues of the flames licked out towards me, as if they were hungry to eat me up. Then Pa opened our door and the flames scurried back and hid under the coals like gleaming eyes.

'Shall I go on?' Walter asked. I squatted down on the rug next to him.

'The puma sprang with a great roar, and Will plunged his sword right into its heart. But the sword broke in two . . .'

'The tweeny has been put in the cats' cage,' I heard Pa say quietly to Ma. Walter hesitated, and we both sat up. Ma was standing with her hand to her mouth. She hated cats. She was terrified of them for some reason.

'What ever for?' she gasped, but Pa realized we were listening and went on with the slow business of unfastening his coat and hanging it up. He wiped the seat of his chair very carefully and went to wind up the gramophone. I nudged Walter with my foot and he began to read again, very quietly and slowly.

'For letting them go,' we heard Pa say, and then the music started and he sat down and closed his eyes.

Walter stared down at his writing book and then closed it up and sat on it. I looked at him and said nothing. Perhaps he was wondering how to finish his story. Ma sat down at the table, staring in front of her. There was an awful, thinking silence in the room.

'Cats are more important than people, it seems,' Pa said out loud, when the music came to an end. Ma helped him on with his coat and stood at the door, watching him walk off across the dark grass. I was looking at the scratch on Walter's hand. There was no need to say anything, I just knew. Ma turned back into the room, shaking her head.

'I can't believe it,' she said, more to herself than to us. 'That wicked woman.'

'I think I'll just go and see Rufus,' Walter muttered. He pulled on his cap and wound his muffler round his neck and was out of the door before Ma could stop him.

'I want you back in half an hour,' she shouted.

I could hardly wait for him to come back, and when he did he was without his muffler and gloves. I noticed, even if Ma didn't. He went straight upstairs and I ran up after him.

'What are you going to do?' I demanded.

'What d'you mean?'

'That's a cat scratch, Walter Hollins.'

He sat down on the bed, nursing his hand. 'It wasn't me. We were all in the cat cage, but I didn't leave it open.'

'Who did then? Stupied Rufus?'

'Nobody did.'

I just sat and stared at him, waiting for him to speak.

'We did shut it, that's what Rufus says.'

I still didn't say anything.

'And Rufus says he didn't go in at all anyway.'

Ma shouted up to us to get ready for bed. Walter sat on the clothes chest and started to unbutton his shirt.

'I w-went down to see Ter-Tweeny,' he said.

It's that stammer of his. If anything's a giveaway, that stammer is. It only happens when he's nervous, and why should he be nervous with me?

'Is she all right?'

'I der-didn't speak to her.'

I knew what he'd done. He'd have shoved his muffler and gloves through the cage mesh and run for it.

'Someone else was there, trying to open the door.'

'Ah,' I nodded. 'That would be Joan probably.'

'No, it was-wasn't.' Walter gulped. 'It w-was Master George.

Something Was Troubling Me

My sister Victoria is getting worse. At first, when our mother died, she just took over the job of being Mistress of the house as if it was a tiresome task that had to be done, though she was pretty strict with the servants. Father stayed away and left her to it. Then she dismissed Nanny and I didn't know what to do with myself. Nanny was always there whenever I needed her. Then when Father went to Australia and Caroline ran away with the Squirrel, Victoria just seemed to make up her mind that she was going to be as unkind as possible to everybody.

The tweeny just fell into her trap. I don't know whether the girl left the cage open or not. It was very careless of her if she did, but maybe she did it on purpose, who knows? It always struck me as one of Victoria's strangest whims, to keep those cats in a cage. But to lock the servant girl in instead! That was madness. But I daren't say anything to my sister, in case she decided to lock me in my schoolroom. She's done that before now. I could write a letter to my father about it, but it would be months before it reached him.

But I thought about the girl all evening. It was cold

outside – I could hear the wind howling down the great chimneys, and it was enough to make me shiver just to think about her. So after the evening meal with my tutor, I decided to go down to the cage and release her. She could go back in next morning and Victoria would never know. I wasn't going to just let her freeze to death because of a careless mistake. As soon as it was dark I went down to the lawn. I could hear someone speaking, and made out that it was the cook and that she had brought the tweeny a bottle of warm tea.

I kept myself hidden. It was better to pretend that I knew nothing about this, in case Victoria found out. And I didn't want the servants to know I was going against my sister. But I couldn't understand why Joan didn't simply open the door and let the girl go. That was what I planned to do. As soon as she had gone I ran across the field and pressed the latch on the cage door. It wouldn't move.

'Who is it now?' I heard the tweeny ask. It was too dark to see her. I kept myself quiet because I didn't want her to know it was me. I tried to force the door.

'It won't open,' she said. 'Miss Victoria made Timothy put a padlock on it, and she's got the key.'

'Ah!' I sighed. It was hopeless. There was nothing I could do to help her. I made my voice as rough as possible so she would think I was one of the farm labourers. 'Are you warm enough?'

She was quiet for a long time, as if she was trying to work out what to say. 'I could do with a nice, warm, velvet jacket.' Without another thought I pulled mine off and tried to push it through the mesh to her. It was impossible.

I turned away, deeply disappointed that I could do nothing at all to help her, and then she said, with a brave, bright sort of laugh in her voice, 'I'll be all right. I've got plenty of blankets here. Timothy brought a pile down when he fixed the padlock, and everyone's been bringing me stuff. If only the gentry knew! It's like Christmas! But ta for trying.'

I felt wretched leaving her, all the same. Hollins opened the door to me and looked at me strangely as I walked past him in my shirt sleeves with my jacket over my arm. It was that look of his that made me think of Walter. Something was troubling me.

It was all working its way round in my head as I went upstairs, and I was remembering what I had seen when I sat up in the tree with Dorothy earlier that day. I remembered Walter running below us, laughing and full of excitement and making silly yowling noises. I remembered the little dark-haired boy riding on the shoulders of the loud boy from the Holts' estate. Clearly I remembered the way he had his leg sticking out to the side, and how there was a gash in it from knee to ankle. What on earth could have caused it, and why was it bothering me now?

I was in bed before I realized. It was a cat scratch, surely? What if those boys had been playing in the cage! Could they have left it open? If I told my sister, what kind of trouble would Walter get into? I lay awake all night, tossing and turning. Would I be blamed too?

How I wished Nanny was there still sleeping in my schoolroom next door. Nanny would have told me what to do.

Dorothy

We've Come About the Cage

*N*o, Walter and I didn't sleep a wink that night. We were glad when morning came and we could get up and get dressed. We couldn't face breakfast, either of us. Walter felt sick for Tweeny, and I felt sick for him. I knew what was on his mind. We told Ma we needed to get to school early and then as soon as we were outside our door I turned to face Walter, but I didn't have to say a word. I could tell by his eyes that he'd made up his mind.

'I'll come with you,' I said. I would have to speak for him, you see.

We went up together to the main door of the Big House and Walter reached up and pulled at the bell. It seemed to clang for ever. To our great relief it wasn't Pa who opened the door, but Timothy. He looked at us with surprise and puzzlement in his knobby brown eyes. 'Back door, Twins,' he said, jerking his head at us like a pigeon.

Walter choked on his first word.

'We need to speak to Miss Victoria,' I said for him. 'It's very important.'

I had once heard Wiley say to Ma that Timothy's brain was no bigger than a rabbit's, and I'm quite sure this was true, because he kept repeating the words to himself as if they were brand new and he'd never come across them before.

'Important!' he said at last, and he stepped back, and we were in! The hall was choky with the smell of polish and woodsmoke. There was a big fire burning in the grate and sending sparks of light everywhere from its reflection in the chandelier. And all the walls were covered in paintings of old gentlemen. I thought it all looked lovely. Timothy led the way along a panelled corridor. I reached out for Walter's hand and he gripped it in mine, and we followed slowly past all the paintings.

We could hear Timothy at the end of the corridor, whispering to someone, and when we reached the top, there was Pa, looking at us more sternly than he had ever done in our lives. But he didn't send us back home and he didn't ask us what we were doing walking round the Big House. And do you know, I think he knew why we had come. And there was something else then I thought about for the first time – what would happen to his job now?

He opened a door and stood with his hands behind his back and said, 'If you please, Miss Victoria, the Hollins twins would like a word with you.'

I thought I would die of fright. I didn't know anything beyond the cold, startled look in the Wicked Sister's eyes. She was sitting at a writing desk with a pen poised in her hand, and at that moment I believed that the nib was as sharp as a dagger.

'Come here, where I can see you.'

We edged forward. Walter kept giving quick little nervous coughs, trying to clear his throat.

'Well?'

'We've come about the cage.' I thought I was going to faint away.

'The cage?'

'The cat cage, Miss Victoria.'

'And?'

And, to my amazement, Walter spoke up. He didn't stammer once. 'This has nothing to do with Dorothy, Miss Victoria. It wasn't Tweeny who left the cage door open. It was me.'

Miss Victoria stared at us. I could see the pinchy skin round her eyes going tight and pale. Ink dribbled down the pen on to her white fingers and she didn't even notice.

'Is this true, Hollins?'

So Pa was still there. I remembered then that he had to stay in a room until he was dismissed. The thought of him having to listen to this made me want to cry. But it wasn't Pa who answered, it was Master George. I hadn't seen him till then, but he came out of a little library room just next to Miss Victoria's writing desk, with a pile of books in his arms. 'Walter's my friend, Victoria. I showed him where the cage was.' He kept his eyes on us, but he didn't smile and nor did we.

Miss Victoria stared at Master George, then at Walter. She looked down at her inky fingers and wiped them on her dress as if she didn't know what on earth she was doing.

'Get to your lessons,' she said at last, without looking at Master George, and he walked quickly out of the room. 'Take the twins away, Hollins. Deal with them as they deserve, and never allow them to come to the house again.'

I went to follow Walter out of the room. Miss Victoria tore up the blotted letter in front of her then looked up, angry, realizing my father was still standing there.

'You are dismissed, Hollins.'

'The tweeny, Miss Victoria?' my father said.

'Leave her there till lunch-time. Servants must learn to know their place.'

'Yes, Miss Victoria.'

In absolute silence, as if he didn't know us, Pa led us down the corridor to Timothy, and it was Timothy who showed us out of the door. We ran all the way down to the lane, and Salty whoahed at us and gave us a lift to school. But he couldn't get a word out of either of us that day.

When we arrived home, Wiley was having tea with Ma. She sat spraying crumbs out of her mouth and not caring whether we were listening or not, she was so full of the story of Miss Victoria changing her mind and letting Tweeny go on the stroke of twelve.

'I expect the poor child was crying her eyes out by then,' said Ma.

'On the contrary! She stalked up to the House like a young Amazon, and took up her tasks with thunder in her eyes. She's a spirited girl, I'll say that for her. She has a

clear conscience, I warrant you that. Not guilty, me lud!'
And Wiley went on to tell Ma the even more interesting
story of finicky Miss Victoria having ink stains all over
her dress.

We were in the garden when Pa came home and we
stayed there until Ma called us in. We could hear the
mumble of his voice, and hers raised in surprise, and then
we were called in. We knew by her face that Pa had told
her everything.

'Eh, Walter Hollins, what are we to do with you?' she
said, and her voice was sad and her eyes were bright. I
knew what she was looking at. Behind us, hanging on
a hook by the door, was the leather strap. Ma had never
used it on either of us, but there it was, a daily reminder
to us that crime would be punished.

Pa came right up to us and put both his hands on
Walter's shoulders. He looked at him for a long time
before he said anything. 'Walter stood in front of Miss
Victoria and spoke up, clear as a bell,' he said at last.
'He'll never stammer again now.'

And we understood by those words that we were
strangely forgiven, that the matter was over as far as he
was concerned, and that we were spared the strap.

'It's Tweeny I'm sorry for. Give her this from me.' Ma
took a warm cake from the range top and wrapped it in a
striped cloth. 'It was meant for the twins' supper, but it'll
do them no harm to go without.'

'And give her this,' I said. I pulled my ribbon out of my
hair. It was my favourite blue one.

'When d'you think she'll be able to wear that?' said Ma, amused, but she wrapped it round her finger to make a ball of it. 'She's only allowed black.'

'She'll wear it at night,' I said.

'She might. It'll be a lovely thing for her to have.' Ma tied it round the cake bundle.

'I'll give her a story!' Walter ran upstairs to tear a page out of his book. When he held it out to Pa his hand was shaking. Oh, Walter! It was 'The Ghost in the Garden'. His best story!

'The poor girl can't read,' Pa said, but all the same he took it and put it into the pocket of his tails, and it was wonderful, watching him going back to the house with our presents. Everything was all right again. Or at least, that's how it seemed.

The Revenge of the Wicked Sister

*N*ext day was Saturday, and after our chores for Ma we ran out to climb our tree, hoping that Master George would come. But we discovered then that everything was not all right, and that nothing would ever be the same again.

As we climbed, Walter told me he had an idea for a story about how Will Tanner might have taken his revenge on the Wicked Witch of Mossley Hill. He had that dreamy look on his face, when he doesn't really listen to what anyone's saying to him because he's too busy listening to the voices in his head. I know him. He put his hand into the box to bring his book out, and instead he found a letter there. He stared at it with his mouth open. I nearly fell off the branch trying to snatch it off him.

Dear Twins,
You were both exceedingly brave to face my sister – you, Walter, for taking the blame for a crime for which you could be only partially responsible, and you, Dorothy, for appearing to be involved when I for one knew that you

could not have been. I don't regret my effort to match your courage, but I'm sorry to say that my sister persuaded my tutor to beat me for my supposed part in it, a task which he enjoyed greatly and I not at all.

Walter put the letter down. 'I wish he'd use proper words.'

I snatched the paper from him. 'They are proper words. You should know them if you're going to be a writer.' I carried on reading. ' "Victoria said that your father would ensure that you would be similarly punished. Dorothy, I hope your beating did not make you cry." Oh, poor Master George, it's not fair! "But that punishment has been succeeded by another, far greater. I have been forbidden ever to see you again." Oh, no!'

Walter took the letter back from me. ' "My tutor is to stay with me at all times, which I can assure you has made him sourer than ever. I cannot imagine how I will spend my time without you. Your friend, Master George.' "

We read the letter again.

'The revenge of the Wicked Sister,' Walter said.

'It sounds like a title for your story. Write it down before you forget it.'

Walter took his notebook out of the tin. 'We ought to write to Master George first. What should we say to him?'

'Dear Master George,' I dictated. 'We're sorry you got hit. We didn't, but Pa is very kind and Ma sent our cake to Tweeny.'

He read it back to me. It didn't sound very much so I scribbled at the bottom, 'We wish we could see you again', folded it up and put it in the tin.

'How's he going to get it though?' I asked.

'How the heck did his letter get here?'

We imagined the glassy-eyed new tutor scrambling up the tree and the very idea made us giggle. We had seen him in church, puffed up and waddly like a black and white duck. But there was nothing else we could do. Pa wouldn't take it for us, we knew that. And we certainly wouldn't dare go anywhere near the Big House again. So we posted our letter in the tin and never believed for a moment that anyone would come for it. We left it for two days before looking again, though we kept peering out of the bedroom window at the tree, looking for a postman of some sort. When we just couldn't bear it any longer we ran to the tree, fighting to be the first to climb it. I won.

'There's a letter! There's a letter!' I shouted. I read it quickly and floated it down to Walter. All it said was that Master George was bored without us.

'Ask him how it got there!' Walter shouted up, and I scrawled on a tiny bit of paper, 'Not much fun with only Walter to play with. Who posts your letters for you?' and slipped it into the tin.

When I slid down the tree I tore my stocking, and this time I knew Ma would be angry. It didn't seem to matter how dirty or wet or bedraggled Walter got, she always forgave him because he was a boy. And I was right. My punishment, as well as darning my stocking, was to put on Ma's working apron and to black-lead the stove. It took me all afternoon and by the end of it I had to be scrubbed clean in the tin bath in front of the fire.

Ma said, 'Keep your feet on the ground in future. One day very soon you're going to look at that tree and ask yourself whatever got into your head to make you want to climb that thing. You will, Dorothy.'

But I thought, no, Ma, I won't. If that's what growing up means, then I don't want to grow up.

Even so, I tried to please her, and let Walter do the letter-collecting for us both. But one day I just had to give in to temptation and that was how I found out who the messenger was.

Walter was at choir with Harry. I'd been to the shop for Ma and, as always, I just looked across at the tree as I came to our gate. I was sure I could see something white bobbing about up in the branches. I ran up to it and from where I was standing I could see a pair of black boots feeling their way down the trunk. My heart started pumping. What if it was Master George? But soon I knew that it was a girl. She slid the last few feet and turned to face me, her pleated cap pulled over her eye and her hair all over the place. It was Tweeny.

Even a Tweeny Can Climb a Tree

Where I come from, there's no such things as trees. All chopped down for firewood! And when I first come to the House I saw these great galumphing things and I thought, I like them. They're like big, kind people, all nodding and whispering to each other and holding out their arms. And that one with the great branches spreading out sideways is just like a big ship.

One day I sneaked down the drive to have a look at it, just to listen to the way the leaves talk to each other. I looked up and what did I see but three pairs of boots sticking out of it! I'd know Master George's boots anywhere – I have to polish them. And the others were just alike, and I bet to meself that they belonged to them Hollins twins.

Lucky things, I thought. Lucky, lucky things, I bet it's the best place in the world, up there. I never thought I'd get the chance to climb it, ever. I never thought I'd have the nerve. Soft me.

The day after Timothy let me out of that cage he come looking for me when I was scrubbing the cellar steps. No, the horse wasn't rocking, if you want to know. That only happens at nights. Timothy knelt down and give me a note.

'It's from Master George,' he whispers, and I looked at him soft like, because why would Master George be writing to me, and what good would it do anyway, seeing as I can't read? 'For the twins,' Timothy said, and I was still puzzled, me.

Give it to their dad then, you big pigeon, I was thinking. Then Timothy winked and he says, 'Time you was feeding them cats, isn't it?' And I'm just about to say 'You daft clothes-peg, there's no cats left!' when we heard Bains clattering about and Timothy darted off, nearly choking himself with excitement.

Well, I thought. I took the pail of mucky water out and emptied it in the yard and I'm thinking, it's true, there's no cats left, but no one's give me nothing to do instead for the next half-hour. And I thought, Master George was real kind, coming out to me that night when I was stuck in that cage, trying to shove his jacket through to me, even if he did pretend he was a field lad. And I knew he'd been shut up in that schoolroom of his, and I thought, I bet he hasn't got no friends, except for them Hollins twins. And I thought, anything I can do to get me own back on that Miss Victoria is worth risking me skin for.

All that thinking! Me brain was working that fast I nearly went into a flat spin. Then I remembered that big huge tree where they was sitting that day. I run straight there, but there wasn't nobody up it. And I thought, if

Miss Dorothy can do it, and she looks as if a fly could knock her over, then so can I! So I climbed it! I climbed the tree! I nearly scared the wits out of meself, but I did it and I wanted to shout me head off when I got to the big sitting-branch bit! Even a tweeny can climb a tree, I wanted to shout. Look at me!

Eh, but I still had that message, didn't I? I saw this tin and I shoved the letter in it and skimbled back down quick and ran to the House. Fancy, no one had missed me! Well, next day Timothy found me again and asked me if I had a message for Master George, and I run back to the tree and skimbled up it again, and there it was. Eh, it's a magic feeling, this. I'm needed, you know what I mean?

But this new letter from Master George – I've got a bad feeling about it. There's misery in the House today. None of the servants seem to know what's going on up there, but I tell you, I wouldn't want to be reading this letter. I would not.

The Liverpool Lady *Has Gone Down*

*T*weeny was right. It was bad news. I waited till Walter came home and we read it together, crouched up on our bed.

Dear Twins.
I can hardly put pen to paper. My tutor has told me that there is news of my father, and that it is not good. He does not yet have all the details, so he cannot tell me more. Can you imagine how tantalizing that is? Believe me, I am beside myself with curiosity and apprehension.

'Whatever that's supposed to mean,' Walter added. 'I wish he'd talk like a person instead of like a book.'
'He can't help it,' I said. 'He's upset.'
When we went downstairs, Ma was sitting at the table and said nothing to us at all. What ever news there was from the Big House had already reached her, that was obvious, but she wasn't going to talk to us about it. It must have been something really awful then. It was Harry who told us. When he came home from work he just

jumped off his bike and left it to clatter on the stones, wheels spinning, and dashed in, full of it all.

'Guess what!' he shouted, and Ma darted him a warning look. He couldn't contain himself. 'The *Liverpool Lady* has gone down off the coast of Italy!'

It meant nothing to me, but Walter recognized the name immediately. 'That's the Master's new ship!' He went deathly white then, and ran outside. I knew where he was going. I followed him up and sat with him on our branch, as still and silent as he was, staring out at the shimmering line of the Mersey. The sky began to grow dim and the river was a deep crimson as though the setting sun was bleeding into it. Cargo ships drifted towards the docks. A big liner was coming in slowly, black and proud against the skyline, with its pilot ship leading the way past the sand bars. It could have been the *Liverpool Lady* coming back from Australia with all her passengers crowding the decks for their first view of Liverpool. But they were all drowned, all the men and women and children, all the sailors, all the animals down below, all the packages and presents and cargo, the teas and the spices and the bars of gold, the rats and the spiders, all gone down to that deep quiet on the bed of the ocean.

And it wasn't the end of the bad news, though nothing could be worse than that, could it? When we went back home, Harry was telling Ma that he might be out of a job. He was a clerk now in the very firm that the Master ran. 'They've got insurance people investigating the accounts. It might be the end of the company, that's what I've heard.'

'Why?' Walter asked, and Ma shushed him up and went out, folding her arms inside her shawl. She wanted to walk under the trees on her own, I think, to let all these awful things settle inside her. We turned straight to Harry for more news.

'All the Master's money was invested in that ship,' Harry explained to us, though I can't say it made any sense. 'If it wasn't fully insured then it's the end of the shipping line, the end of my job.'

But it wasn't till we were in bed that night and we heard Pa talking to Ma downstairs that we knew the very worst bit of the story. It seemed that the Master had been returning to England on the *Liverpool Lady* when she sank.

Dear, Plump, Gossipy Nanny

Victoria asked for me to be sent to the morning room straight after breakfast. I had lain awake all night, thinking of what my tutor had told me and wondering what it could mean. I had read and re-read the letter my father had sent me, and that had been so full of joy and optimism that I couldn't imagine what could have gone wrong to spoil it all. Unless Miss Greenaway had refused his offer of marriage after all! Yes, I decided. That would be it. And I can't say I was sorry. Maybe it would bring him home to me.

Yet why was there such an air of misery in the house? I had been released from my schoolroom, and my tutor had been unaccountably reading in the library all day as if he had forgotten that he was supposed to be testing my verbs. I didn't trouble to remind him, but all the same, I was quite pleased when Victoria sent for me and I knew that I would be finding out at last what all the mystery was about.

When I went into the morning room she was standing looking out across the gardens, and her deep silence made my heart beat with slow dread. Hercules was pulling the great roller across the lawn, with Nat leading him. I should have liked to climb on Hercules's back and ridden away from the Estate forever, and never have to listen to what my sister was going to tell me.

Victoria gave Hollins the signal to withdraw and I knew that it was a private family matter that was to be discussed.

'George, the *Liverpool Lady* has gone down.' Victoria's voice was very low and steady. She was still looking at Hercules. My heart went as still as stone inside me. It couldn't be true. Surely not. My father's beautiful ship, his dream of dreams. Surely it couldn't be true. When Victoria turned round I could not see her face because the light behind her was so strong, but now I could hear a crack in her voice. 'We believe that Father was among the passengers.'

I could not register any of this. None of her words made sense. I wanted to fling them away like pebbles spinning across water. I had Father's letter in my pocket, warm still. He had not said anything in it about returning home so soon. She must be mistaken.

'He sent me a letter by packet ship,' she went on. 'It was to be kept as a surprise for you, George. You may read it. It arrived three days ago.'

And I was still staring at her, unable to say anything, or to take in a word of what she was saying. She picked up a note that was indeed in my father's handwriting and came towards me with it, then put a hand on my shoulder, and I saw then that her eyes were red and raw with crying, and I felt I did not know my harsh sister any more.

'I have sent for Nanny,' she said, 'and have asked her to spend the day with you. She will be upstairs in the schoolroom now, waiting.'

I snatched the letter out of her hand and ran out of the room, but halfway up the stairs I just had to stop and read it. I had to know for sure. I scanned the page and the letters jumped and bubbled like insects. I could hardly take them in, but I could hear Father's voice in every word.

Have decided to return with the ship and her valuable cargo. There is a packet ship which will bring this letter to you speedily, but I will follow . . . had not intended to return so soon . . . unexpected . . . but keep it as a surprise for George . . . your loving father.

Dear, plump, gossipy Nanny was waiting for me in the schoolroom, her face creased with worry for me. I had not seen her for four years. She put her arms round me just as she used to when I was a small boy, and let me cry and cried with me until there were no tears left.

Tweeny

Walking into Nothing

*I*t happened again that night. I always know it's happening because it wakes me up, this creak, creak, creak right under me ear. It's because I sleep in the kitchen and the noise is down in the cellar. Usually I try to ignore it, but that night, with all them goings-on with them gentry upstairs, I just couldn't. Me heart wouldn't let me. So I pulled me shawl round me shoulders and took a candle and crept down the steps. It's like going into a cave down there, it's that cold and damp and dark. It's like walking into nothing.

And there he was, Master George, rocking backwards and forwards, backwards and forwards on his old wooden horse. His eyes was wide open, but seeing nothing, if you know what I mean. Fast asleep with his eyes open. It was no secret to us servants that he sleepwalked. Joan told me if I ever saw him doing it I was to leave him be. I knew it was dangerous to wake him up. When he'd finished he just climbed down off the horse and stroked it. Then he spoke. 'Goodbye,' it sounded like. Nothing more. Then he glided past me like a ghost and went back up all them stairs to his bed.

Dorothy

I Have a Plan . . .

*W*alter and I didn't expect to hear from Master George again. His world was a dark, deep hole now and we didn't know how to talk about it or how to think about it. Yet there was a letter for us next day. We saw Tweeny by the tree and ran up to her to save her the climb.

' "Dear Twins," ' I read out loud. I knew that Tweeny was hanging round to listen but I was so eager to read it that I forgot that she was only a servant. ' "I have a plan which I must discuss with you urgently. Would you agree to meet me in Our Place at six o'clock?" '

That was all. 'A plan?' said Walter. 'What does he mean?'

Tweeny just shook her head and shrugged. 'Don't ask me,' she said. 'I've not seen sight nor sound of any of the gentry. Timothy give me the note and said to take it quick because Master George was all of a dither.'

'I'm not surprised,' I said.

'So what have I to tell him?'

'Tell Timothy to tell him "yes", Walter said. 'We haven't got time to write to him.'

Salty met us running along Rose Lane and leaned down from his cart to talk to us.

'I hear there's bad news at the House,' he said. He shook his head and snorted, just like Elijah. 'It doesn't matter how high they are in the world; when they fall, they fall, same as everyone. Death comes to us all.' He intoned it mournfully, like the great bell at church.

We clopped along in silence, and I was looking at the yellow catkins unfurling from the branches of the pussy-willow trees as we passed under them, and thinking it didn't seem right, somehow, that there was so much sunshine about that day, as if the world didn't care.

At school Miss Brogan made us all pray for the lost souls of the *Liverpool Lady*, and because we were connected with the ship the other children kept looking at us. I glanced sideways at Walter and knew that he felt as I did, a bit proud, a bit special. It was strange to be feeling that way and I didn't understand it but I couldn't help it. I hung my head and tried to remember the Master. I couldn't. It was as if his memory had slipped away. All I could think about was Master George and what his Great Plan might be.

Ma wouldn't let me go out that night until I'd helped her with the ironing. I could have burst with disappointment. As soon as Walter had gone out I asked her the question that was burning in my head.

'Ma . . . could Master George come and live with us?'

Ma banged down the heavy iron in surprise. 'Dorothy, what on earth are you thinking of! Here we are squashed up in two rooms, and he's living in the lap of luxury! How could he live here?'

'I think he'd prefer it, all the same.'

'Well,' said Ma, thumping the last folded sheet on the pile. 'I'm sure you're right. But it couldn't be done. Things like that just don't happen in this world. There's a place for them and there's a place for us. I'm not saying I don't feel sorry for him. My heart goes out to the young Master, it really does. But there's nothing we can do to help him.'

So that was the end of my little plan. Yes, it was ridiculous, I see it now. But Master George had an even wilder plan of his own.

When I arrived, he and Walter were sitting side by side with their hands round their knees, saying nothing, both staring out to the river. I squirmed up on to my perch against the trunk. A blackbird was singing over our heads as if it was the best day in the world. Out on the river a tugboat hooted, then another, and then we just had silence. I wanted to tell Master George how sorry I was, but I was shy suddenly. I just didn't know what words to use. So he was the first one to speak and what he said was the biggest shock of all.

'Daw, I'm going to Australia.'

That made me blush a little, because although Walter sometimes called me Daw nobody else did. It warmed me up, hearing Master George say it and for a second I didn't take in what else he'd said.

'I want to find my father.'

'But I thought . . . we heard . . .' Now I really was embarrassed. Hadn't Master George heard the news?

'I can't believe he's drowned, Daw.' His voice trembled slightly and I could feel my tears starting up for him. 'But even if he's not there . . . even if he really is dead – ' He paused and the silence was long and deep and awful – 'I want to do what he asked me to do, and keep the family name going in Australia.'

I looked at Walter. It sounded so brave and good. So possible.

'And I want to find Miss Greenaway. I can't stay here if Father isn't coming back. Not with Victoria.'

We were all startled to hear a snort of agreement coming from the branches below us.

'What's that?' Walter asked. There was silence from the tree. Walter swung himself round so he was hanging upside down. I don't know how he does that. When he pulled himself back up again all the blood had run to his head, so his face was scarlet.

'It's Tweeny!' he whispered.

'Spying on us!' I was indignant. 'Tell her to go away, Master George.'

'I'm only doing what tweenies do all the time!' Her voice floated up, pleading. 'Just listening in, that's all. I won't tell no one. Any road, I've got an idea for Master George.'

He looked at us and tapped his knuckles together, as if he couldn't think what to do about her. He might be the Master's son, but he wasn't really used to ordering people about.

'Come up here, Tweeny,' he said.

There was a bit of scrabbling and then up she came, her cheeks hectic like red poppies and her hair tumbling out of her cap over her shoulders. Gypsy hair, Ma would have called it. I wish mine was like that. I don't know how we managed to squeeze on to the branch together, the four of us. Master George put out his hand to steady Tweeny, and I felt a tug of jealousy.

'It's about going to this osty-wotsit place,' she said. She didn't look at him, but at Walter. 'Tell Master George I've got an idea. He can go on a boat.'

I raised my eyebrows at Walter and he smiled at me quickly. 'We know that, Tweeny. There's no other way.'

'Trouble is, it costs twenty guineas,' Master George said. 'And I don't have any money.'

'You're supposed to be the rich one!' Walter reminded him. 'Twenty guineas though! I could borrow a couple of bob off our Harry.'

Master George shook his head. 'I'm going to stow away with the cargo.'

'But you'd be there for months! How would you eat? And there'd be rats . . . and . . . tarantulas!'

Tweeny stopped me. 'He doesn't have to do that. Tell him to get a job as a cabin boy. That's how me brother went to America. That's what I wanted to tell him.'

'A cabin boy!' said Walter. 'But that's a servant!'

Far below us, an open-topped car was making its way to the House. We could see Miss Caroline sitting in it, a handkerchief up to her face. Our excitement sobered down. The terrible news was so fresh to us, and yet already we had put it somewhere else, as if it was too big for us to think about.

'Ask Master George if he'll please excuse me,' Tweeny said. 'There's going to be gentry coming all night, and I should be doing the fires.'

'Yes, you go, Tweeny,' Master George murmured. He sounded as if his thoughts were miles away. 'And I must go and greet my sister.'

We all slid down the tree and ran off in our various directions, all full of things to think about. Walter saw Nat and ran off to talk to him. The sky was settling down for the night and the lamps were being lit in the Big House, casting a glow around it. We would soon be called in for bed. But I didn't want to go in yet. I wandered down the track by the wall and out on to Bark Hill Road. I could see a bicycle nudging its way along it.

'Harry!' I shouted, and waved both my hands in the air. He put his head down and pedalled as fast as he could towards me, showing off a bit. I climbed in front of him and rode the rest of the way, my legs sticking out at either side and my skirt hoisted clear of the wheels. Ma would have sent me straight to bed for that. But I was bursting with excitement now. If anyone could help Master George, it was Harry.

A Grand and Glorious Thing To Do

In two days Harry had come home with the news we wanted. He whispered it to us when we were in bed.

'There's a ship called the *Olympia* leaving for Australia in three days' time,' he said. 'She's leaving early with all the people who were supposed to be going on the *Liverpool Lady*. Captain Wild has put up a poster asking for more crew.'

'Cabin boys?' I whispered. I could hardly get the words out, my heart was thumping so much.

'Definitely. Signing them on tomorrow afternoon.'

Walter wanted to get up straight away and take a message to Master George, but I wouldn't let him. 'It's too dangerous,' I whispered. 'No one must find out, Walter.'

'I'll keep your secret, if you'll keep mine,' Harry said. 'I'm going to join the Army. Only don't tell Ma yet. If the war starts, I'm going to go and fight for our country.'

We lay back, thinking hard. Harry was already snuffling into sleep. His news would keep. It was too big to think about yet, though at church we had to pray that the war wouldn't happen. But what would Ma say if Harry went to be a soldier? Downstairs, she was making bread for tomorrow's breakfast, and she was singing quietly to herself. She would come up to bed soon. I tried to concentrate on our big plan.

'Walter,' I said suddenly, 'they'll be able to tell Master George is gentry because of his clothes!'

'That's what I was thinking. And his voice – he's so la-di-dah.'

'They'd never give a gentleman's son a cabin boy's job. I'll have to sort him out.' I got out of bed and rummaged in the clothes chest. There was that old, patched suit of Harry's that was waiting for Walter to grow into. I pulled it out quickly, stuffed it into a bolster case and shoved it under our mattress just as Ma was climbing the stairs.

'That's his clothes seen to,' I said. 'You'll have to give him elocution lessons!'

We were both giggling as Ma was getting undressed in the dark. 'What's got into you two?' she asked. 'Laughing at a time like this, with the Big House in mourning for the Master!' For some reason, that made things even funnier. I think it was nerves. We never stopped for a minute to wonder whether we were doing the right thing or whether Master George should be helped to run away like that. It just seemed, at the time, a grand and glorious thing to do, to send him off to the other side of the world to start a new life.

It was a good thing there was no school next day. Walter surprised Ma by offering to run to ask Nat if there was any early rhubarb we could have. He came back, panting and triumphant, with ten pink rhubarb sticks under his arm. But the best thing was he had managed to pass a note to Tweeny while she was feeding the hens. We had asked Master George to meet us by the main gates after lunch. If he was there, we would just have time to catch the tram down to the docks. We had our church collection pennies ready for the fare, and I had the bolster of clothes. But he mustn't be late.

He was there on time, tense, pacing up and down with his hands behind his back. I gave him the clothes and he went off into the bushes to change. Walter kept guard and I ran up and down the lane in an agony of waiting. I just couldn't keep still and Master George seemed to take for ever. When he emerged at last he was unrecognizable. He even walked differently, on account of Harry's boots being a bit tight for him.

'How do I look?' he asked.

'He'll do fine,' came Tweeny's voice from somewhere. 'But tell him his accent's like toffee.' She scrambled out from under a laurel bush, pinker and brighter than ever. 'I'm sorry if I'm being nosy but it's got to come right for him, hasn't it?' And she looked at Master George with such understanding and pity in her eyes that I could feel myself blushing for her. I wanted him to know that I was just as worried about him as she was, but I didn't know how to make my eyes talk the way she did.

And then she took a deep breath and said something that she'd obviously been rehearsing all morning. She said it to me, but it was meant for Master George. 'I don't want to stay here any more than Master George does, not if that sister of his is going to be in charge all the time, and I hope he'll excuse us for saying that. And I can't go back home because there's eleven children to look after there and it's not my fault and I don't want to do it. My dad isn't like yours, Twins. He's cruel and nasty and I don't want nothing more to do with him. So what I want to say is this – ask Master George to take me with him!'

Walter had Master George's clothes in the big bolster and he was swinging it backwards and forwards in front of him like the pendulum of a clock. None of us said anything, we just stared at it swinging backwards and forwards, tick-tock tick-tock.

'I could look after him,' Tweeny went on. 'How can he look after himself? And I'll speak up for him. He won't have to open his mouth, not till he's used to the idea of talking common. I'll make out he's me brother! I'll get jobs for us both as cabin boys. I know I can do it.'

'What d'you think, Master George?' I asked him.

'I think it's worth a try, Tweeny, if you're willing,' he said.

'But she's a girl!' Walter protested. 'They'll never take a girl on.'

Tweeny took off her pleated cap then. All that wonderful wild Gypsy hair of hers had gone, cropped short and shaggy. 'I just need some boy's clothes, and then they'll never know,' she said. 'Please, Master Walter. Please.'

'Oh crikey!' You should have seen the look of horror on Walter's face, and a split second later I understood too.

'Well she can't wear those,' I said, pointing at the bolster, 'and there's no time to go back to the cottage for anything. The tram'll be at the corner any minute.'

Tweeny ducked into the bushes again. 'Don't think about it, just do it!' she sang out, bright as a sparrow.

'Poor Walter,' I giggled. 'Go on!'

So Tweeny passed her clothes to me and Walter passed his to Master George, and they were swopped round. And when they'd finished, Walter was the cheekiest-looking little serving-maid I've ever come across, and Tweeny made a very handsome boy.

'I can hear the tram!' I shouted. 'Run and stop it, someone.'

Walter was still the fastest runner, even in a long skirt. He clutched his maid's cap in one hand and pulled it back on as soon as the tram stopped. We panted on board and sat crammed together on one bench. Walter lifted up the hem of his skirt to wipe his sweaty face and I slapped his wrist.

'You could have worn my clothes, Walter,' Master George said suddenly, and they both started laughing then, because not one of us had thought of that before.

'But you're the Master,' I said. 'It wouldn't have been right.'

Harry was on the lookout for us at the docks, and not a flicker of surprise crossed his face when he saw us. He told me afterwards that he thought Walter was Master George's chambermaid, and a very pretty one at that. Walter was never allowed to forget it. Harry jerked his head towards a dingy warehouse and we joined the queue of men who were hoping to be taken on as crew. The docks were piled with stuff waiting for carters and stevedores to load on board, tons and tons of coal, heaps of crates and boxes and barrels stuffed with food and wines. 'Royal Albert Bone China' was written across one of the barrels. I was wondering what it was, and what could be so particular about it that someone wanted to take it all the way to Australia. And suddenly we were in the front of the queue and were being pushed into the warehouse together. Master George and Tweeny stepped forward side by side. The steward hardly looked at them.

'What are we on?' he asked, ticking his pencil down a list. 'Oh yes. Cabin boys. That you?'

'Yes, sir,' said Tweeny quickly. She stood with her legs slightly apart and her hands behind her back, just like Master George. 'Me and me brother.'

I was beginning to shake. Walter sniffed and I passed him my handkerchief.

'Ever been on a boat before?'

Master George nodded.

'Five minutes on a rowing boat and even then he nearly drowned!' Walter whispered behind his hand. The steward looked across at us, tapping his paper with the end of his pen. I thought he looked bored.

'Our big brother is a cabin boy on the *Plymouth*,' Tweeny said.

The steward yawned. 'American line. You don't look over-strong, young man.'

'Oh I am, sir, me. I'm used to carrying great buckets of coal and scrubbing floors and doing all kinds. I've worked hard all me life.'

The steward pushed his papers away and rubbed his eyes. 'All right, lads. We're sailing on tomorrow evening's tide, did you know that?'

They both nodded, glancing at each other, swopping shy excited grins. The steward walked over to the grimy window and peered out of it. 'The boarding houses are crammed with folks wanting to emigrate to Australia. Sooner we get going, sooner we can come back for more. Know about *Liverpool Lady*, do you? A ship can go down, even the best ship. Wouldn't wish a disaster like that on anyone. But Leighton's downfall is our fortune. That's the way of the world.'

Master George had pulled his handkerchief out of his back pocket and was twisting it round in his hands. I thought he would tear it in two.

The steward had his eyes on the rush of the quay outside. Horses were pulling great cartloads of coal for the *Olympia,* hundreds of them one after another in a long patient line. We could hear their drivers shouting and whistling.

'Every inch of the ship will be covered in coal dust by the time that lot's loaded. That's your first job: cleaning, and I expect it to be bright as a new pin. Get here by first light tomorrow, lads. Plenty to do. We're stretched for time as it is. And when we pull away from Liverpool you'll see as good a sight as you'd see anywhere in the world, with them grand new buildings on the skyline. It's a proud, beautiful city. And you won't be clapping eyes on it again, till summer's come and gone.'

He swung round again, as if he was just waking himself up out of a trance. 'Know anyone else wants a job on board?' he asked sharply, and before I knew what was happening Walter was stepping forward with his hand in the air. I hauled him back by the belt of his pinny.

'Sorry, miss,' the steward smiled at him. 'I don't need young ladies.'

'Right, sir,' said Tweeny. 'Thank you, sir.'

As soon as we were outside she let out a shriek of joy and flung her flat cap in the air. 'I'm gettin' away, I'm gettin' away!'

'Would you really have gone to Australia?' I asked Walter.

'I just got carried away. But one day I'll go. I'll find Master George there and buttle for him.'

And we went quiet, suddenly remembering what it was all about, and that we might never see our friend again. Tomorrow he was going. We were all locked into the same thoughts, it seemed, because none of us spoke a word on the way back, though Tweeny's eyes were full of light, and Master George's lips kept working silently as if he was talking to himself, saying important things over and over again.

When we sneaked through the gates and they had changed back into their proper clothes, it was as if we'd all been taking part in a play, and the pretence was over now. But it wasn't a play, was it? It was real. It was really going to happen.

'I don't think you should come with us in the morning,' Master George said. 'It's too risky, with four of us.'

We knew he was right, but we ached to be there on the quayside, waving them off. We stood awkwardly, not knowing how to say goodbye. Then, very stiffly, he shook hands with us. I wanted to cry then, I really did. My throat was a burning hole. Tweeny bobbed to us, a servant girl again. We heard the six o'clock chimes from Mossley Hill Church, and they'd never seemed so cheerless and sad. We turned away and left them.

'I wish we hadn't gone,' I said to Walter as we were running back to our cottage.

He shook his head. 'You can't say that. We're in it now. We couldn't stop him, so we had to help him.'

I nodded, but I felt sick with worry. It didn't seem like an adventure any more. Tweeny would be in deep trouble already for going missing all afternoon. She would probably be dismissed, we all knew that. So the plan had to work, and we knew that we couldn't tell a soul about it till after the *Olympia* had sailed. We'd be at school then. We wouldn't even be able to watch it from our tree.

Tweeny

Free!

Oh la! Bains was raging mad when I got back. I didn't
care. I didn't care what no one said to me or how
they glared at me. I wasn't a servant no more. I know
she'd been good to me in her own way, and I wanted to
say that to her, but I couldn't. How could I tell anyone
about the plans that were bumping about inside of me
head? Not that anyone would care about me, but just
supposing I was followed or something, and they found
out about Master George. Oh no, I wasn't going to spoil
nothing for him. So I kept me mouth shut when all the
other servants went off to bed, and just give Joan a special
smile, that maybe she'd remember when I was gone. Soft,
me. Why should she care?

Could I get to sleep? I lay with me eyes open till I
heard three o'clock chime, and I rolled up me mattress as
quiet as I could. Underneath it were some shabby clothes
Nat had borrowed me. I had to tell him they was for me
brother. I got dressed quick and went out quiet as a cat.
And there at the gates was Master George, waiting for
me. We turned back once to look at the Big House, all
dark and quiet behind the trees, but neither of us said
nothing. What was there to say?

We ran down to the river and began our long walk to the docks. And me heart was singing, singing like a lark. I was free!

Master George

Yes, I Could Do It!

I was glad Tweeny was with me. She had a knack of finding her way round in the dark. I think I'd have lost my nerve and gone back if it hadn't been for her. No, not gone back. I never wanted to go back to Bark Hill again. I left a note of goodbye to my tutor, thanking him for his services. And I looked in on the Dowager, who never seems to sleep.

'Goodbye, Grandmother,' I said. I told her I was going to Australia. I knew there was no problem in telling her that, because even if she remembered in the morning nobody would believe her. But it thrilled me to say it out loud, and it resolved my purpose. She laughed and told me to enjoy myself. Perhaps I would, though it was difficult to imagine enjoying anything much without my father.

As soon as I reached Melbourne I was going to find Miss Greenaway and ask her to take me in. I had been over this in my head a hundred times. Yes, I could do it!

We could hear the noise of the docks from half a mile away. Tired as we were from our long walk, we started running. There were lamps flickering on the *Olympia*, and she looked huger than ever, a floating mansion. The quayside was as busy as if it was the middle of the day, thronging with people and vehicles and horses. Word had got round that the *Olympia* was due to sail, and cabs and coaches were pulling up with people packed in them as tight as herrings in a barrel, with their goods and trunks strapped to the top. Such a clamour of voices and whistling and laughing and yet through it all we heard our steward shouting.

We ran to him, and he set us to work immediately, brushing the decks and carrying barrels and trunks on board. I don't know how Tweeny managed, but I could hardly lift the things. The barrels were easy, they could be rolled, but I didn't have the strength to lift the trunks. I don't think I've ever lifted anything heavier than a book in my life before. I was struggling to lift up a huge strapped basket, hoping no one would see how hard I was finding it, and I heard Tweeny say, 'Eh, give us a shout when you want help.' She smiled at me, and her face was so full of excitement that I couldn't help smiling too. And that was something new, because I've never looked a servant in the face before, apart from Nanny. She lifted up the other end of the basket and we carried it easily together.

Downstairs below deck where we had to take the stuff was so dark we could hardly find our way around. And we were still loading when morning came up with such a rush of gold it was like a flag unfurling. The gulls were sweeping round us with their great laughing cries. 'Away! Away!' they seemed to be calling. 'You're going away!'

Dorothy

Find Master George

I don't know how Walter and I managed to get through our lessons at school that day, I really don't. I kept drawing ships on my slate and having to rub them off quickly when Miss Brogan came round with her flaring nostrils and her horsy eyes. I knew what Walter was doing. I could just tell by the dreamy look on his face. He was thinking up a new Will Tanner story, and I was quite sure it would have something to do with a young prince crossing the perilous seas.

All the way home we were trying to think of ways to sneak off to the quay so we could just see the *Olympia* again. Any minute now it would be leaving, if the tide was right. We didn't have any money for a tram and if we walked there and back it would take ages and Ma would be fretting. We trudged to the gate with a kind of hopeless emptiness inside us. And there was Salty, just pulling out. He waved to us and reined in Elijah.

'Just been up to the House,' he said, 'and Cook told me that young Master George has gone missing in the night. Did you know anything about that?'

Walter looked at me and frowned, surprise written all over his face.

'And Mawks found his velvet suit in an old bolster case under some bushes. What next! Do you suppose he's running round naked?'

I couldn't bring myself to look at Walter. I could hear him hiccuping, trying to keep his breathing steady.

'Who knows what the grieving mind will do?' Salty rumbled. 'I have known people do stranger things than that even, and 'tis nothing more sinister than the woebegone heart crying out for comfort.'

'Dorothy wanted him to come and live with us,' Walter said. 'But Ma said our house was too small for him.'

'Better'n living up there, all the same. Without neither mother nor father, the boy is a lost waif.' Salty wiped his nose on the back of his hand and tightened the reins. 'The tweeny girl is missing too, but that's another matter. She's just had enough of her who's mistress up there. Well, can't stop here ruminating. I have to move on, Twins. Have to deliver to the *Olympia,* what is sailing tonight for Australia.'

Here was our chance and there was no way we would miss it. Walter was already scrambling on to the back of the cart while I was pleading with Salty.

'Please can we come! I missed the *Liverpool Lady* going out because I was in hospital . . . I've never watched a big ship going off to Australia . . . please?'

'Why, there's ships going all the time to Australia and Americee and all them furrin faraway places,' said Salty. 'Specially now there's rumours of war, God help us, and folks is running away. But if you want to come so special today, you're welcome.'

By the time Salty had pulled Elijah's nose out of the rose bush we were both up on the cart. We couldn't believe our luck. But chance is a funny thing, as we were soon to find out. How different everything might have been if we hadn't been able to go to the port that day.

There seemed to be hundreds of people milling round when we arrived, sitting on trunks or kissing each other goodbye. Steerage passengers were already boarding, surging up the gangway like a stream of ants crawling up a twig.

'Funny do, that is!' said Salty. 'Tossing about on the sea in that big barrel for weeks on end and paying good money to do it!'

'Wouldn't you want to go to Australia though, Salty?'
Walter was full of it, I could see.

'I would not,' said Salty. 'God only knows what they eat over there.'

He left us near the port buildings and drove Elijah down to the loading bay. And I was on the tips of my toes trying to look over people's shoulders, when I caught sight of something that made me go cold with dread. It was Miss Victoria, taller than any other woman there, grand and stern in her black coat and bonnet, and with her face set in that white, grim way she had. I could only think of one thing that could have brought her to the docks that day.

There were boys running all over the place, heaving cabin trunks out of carriages and struggling through the crowds to carry them on board. Any one of them could be Master George. Now the second-class passengers were being allowed on board. An old man in front of us clasped his grandchildren to him, tears streaming down his cheeks. 'Goodbye, goodbye,' he kept saying, and his voice was breaking into little pieces. 'Goodbye, goodbye.'

'Never do that,' I said to Walter. 'Promise me you'll never go off to Australia and leave me.'

Very soon now the great ship would be pulling away. It must be the saddest and most exciting thing in the world to be walking up that gangway. I felt it too, felt a pull of wanting to be on board and sailing away out of Liverpool Bay and into the distance. But I would never want to leave Ma.

We were heading for Harry's office when he suddenly tumbled out of the door as if the place was on fire.

'Harry!' we shouted, and he ran over to us, his eyes flashing with anxiety and excitement. He pulled us with him and ran towards the landing stage.

'Find Master George,' he was shouting. 'I've been looking all over for him. He mustn't go to Australia. There's news about the Master. Tell him that. Get him off.'

'Get him off?' I said, as stupid as a hen. I couldn't believe what he was saying.

'How?' asked Walter.

'Find him!' Harry shouted, his voice a wail of despair. And he ran off, shouting, 'Master George! Master George!'

'He means it,' said Walter. He looked up at the great ship and the long gangway that led up to it. 'Let's do it, Dorothy.'

We tagged on to a family with about eight children and while the official was looking at the tickets we just ducked away and ran up to the main deck. Now they were on board no one was in a hurry any more. They were just strolling about on deck, chatting, leaning against the rails, waving their gloves at the watchers below. They were being so annoying, ambling about as if there was all the time in the world. How on earth could the ship hold so many people and not sink? But I didn't have time to worry about that.

'Please let me find him,' I kept muttering, desperate with the urgency of Harry's message. 'Please let me find him.'

I kept losing Walter as he ducked under arms and scrambled over feet, and when I had lost him altogether I grabbed the arm of a man in uniform and asked him where the cabin boys would be.

'In the cabins, I should think,' he said. 'Unpacking trunks.' He waved towards some stairs and I tumbled down them into an inky blackness. I was in a long corridor with what seemed like hundreds of doors leading off it.

'Master George!' I yelled. I didn't care who heard me now. 'Master George? Where are you?'

I opened one of the doors that had a flickering light coming from it, and found a lady being dressed by a maid. She flapped her hand at me as if I was a troublesome fly. I ran off again and at last saw a boy in a smart, blue uniform coming out from a cabin at the other end.

'Wait!' I shouted. He paused and looked over his shoulder, and I saw then that it wasn't a boy at all, but Tweeny.

'Miss Dorothy! Don't tell us you're coming as well!'

'Where's Master George?' I shouted. 'He mustn't go to Australia!'

'What?' she said. 'What are you talking about?'

For the first time, I stopped to question myself. What if this was Miss Victoria's doing? What if she had got the truth out of Harry and made him bring Master George to her?

'You can't stop him now,' Tweeny said. 'His heart's set on it.'

I shook my head. I didn't know what to do. I imagined Harry's face again and saw the urgency in his eyes.

'Please help me to find him,' I said. 'It's about his father. I don't know what to do.'

'God bless you, miss, you're in a state.' Tweeny opened a door, disappeared through it and seemed to be gone for ever. She came back with Master George. He looked as flustered and worried as I felt.

'There's news about your father,' I told him. I could feel all the excitement draining away from me, now that I had found him, now that I had to give him this strange news. 'You mustn't go.'

'My father? My father?' Master George's voice was trembling. He looked at me as if I was trying to play some cruel kind of trick on him, and to tell you the truth I didn't know what I was doing any more.

'Get off quick and find out what it is,' Tweeny said, as familiar to him as if he really was her brother.

And suddenly there was a blast from a hooter that seemed to make the whole boat shake. Master George looked from one to the other of us, stupid with disbelief and confusion.

'Go on!' Tweeny pushed him a little. 'Skedaddle, quick!'

'Tweeny!' I said. 'Aren't you coming with us?'

She shook her head. 'When I stepped out the door of that Big House I stopped being Tweeny. I'm Mary Rogerson, and I'm proud to be me. I'm fourteen years old today. I'm Mary Rogerson, and I'm going to Australia. Now get off quick, the pair of yez, or you'll all be coming with me.'

Then she turned away and went back into the cabin to carry on with her work. Master George stared after her, his face bunched up with worry. God alone knows what he was thinking. Then he turned away and we walked off the ship together, past all the first-class passengers who had just been boarded, down the gangway and back on to the quayside.

I had no idea where Walter might be. The hooter gave another deafening blast and then all of a sudden there he was, racing down the gangway with his arms in the air.

'Wait!' he was shouting. 'I'm coming ashore!'

As soon as he jumped on to the landing stage the

gangway was pulled away. A band started playing 'God Save our Gracious King'.

All around us people were waving handkerchiefs. Smoke poured from the ship's funnels, and the seagulls lifted into the sky like white flags flying. Master George stared up at them, his hands clenched into tight little fists. The long mooring ropes started snaking out from their capstans, and the great ship lumbered away from the quayside.

Oh, what had we done?

The Flight is Ended

I stood there with Dorothy and Walter until the band stopped playing, watching the *Olympia* moving away behind her line of bobbing tugboats. I can't tell you what was going on in my heart then. I had a dream and it had been smashed to pieces. I took off my cabin-boy's cap and stuffed it into my pocket.

'Now what?' I was incapable of making decisions any more. I feared greatly that I had been betrayed. I would never have left the *Olympia* if it had not been for Dorothy. She would not lie to me, I knew that. But had somebody else lied to her?

'I think we should go to the office where Harry works,' Dorothy suggested, and blindly I followed her and Walter. I knew the office well. It was where my father's dream had started, many years ago, and where he had taken me to look at the fresh designs of the *Liverpool Lady*. And as we approached the building the door opened, and out came my sister Victoria. I felt as though my limbs had been weighted with lead. Indeed, indeed, I said to my heart. The flight is ended. But I walked steadily forward, and she, not recognizing me in my uniform, turned aside. And there was someone speaking to her whose voice I recognized.

I rushed forward and flung myself into his arms, and he stepped back, not knowing me for just a second, then put both his arms around me.

'Is it really you, Father?' I kept saying. 'Is it really you?'

Dorothy

If It Hadn't Been for Us

I have never seen a man embrace his son so tenderly, and have never known such happiness for someone else. But we couldn't stay and watch, could we? This wasn't meant for us. We slipped away, Walter and I.

It was the end of the day and the offices were closing. We saw Harry putting on his bicycle clips and went to him. All the worry had gone from his face by now, and he was whistling cheerfully.

'Whew, that was a near one, Twins,' he said.

'Why didn't you tell us the Master was here?' I demanded.

'Because I didn't know. The senior clerk told me that a letter had arrived this morning to say the Master had left the *Liverpool Lady* weeks ago at Aden to do some sightseeing, and had been taken ill there. He was going to take up his journey again by packet-boat. That was all I knew. That was when I went into a blue panic and started charging round trying to find Master George.'

'Crikey!' That was all Walter could say. 'Crikey!'

'Miss Victoria stormed in saying she'd had the same letter and what could we tell her and, blow me, next minute the Master himself walks through the door! He only heard about the *Liverpool Lady* going down when he arrived in Tilbury, and he took a train straight to the office.'

'Crikey!' Walter said again.

'What a day! I could do with a sup of ale, but I suppose you two want a lift home.'

We took it in turns, one riding on his crossbar and one running alongside. We were all talking at the same time, gabbling on about Tweeny and Master George and the Master and the ship. So much had happened in the last couple of hours that it seemed like weeks since we had arrived at the docks.

'If it hadn't been for Salty we'd never have got there,' I told Harry.

'And if I hadn't seen you we might never have found Master George.'

'But then, if it hadn't been for us, he wouldn't have been on the *Olympia* in the first place,' Walter reminded us.

'You should have seen Walter rushing down the gangway!' I burst out, and our voices were laughing and singing along the dim and echoey lane, when we saw a strange procession heading towards us. All the servants of the house, led by Pa with his lantern on a pole, were walking in a tired bunch. They stopped still when they saw us coming.

Pa called out to us, 'Is that the twins?' And it suddenly occurred to us that we would have been expected home ages ago. Used as she was to us playing in the fields and lanes for all hours, Ma would never have expected us to miss our tea.

Pa and the servants were all round us in a second, full of crossness and relief and worry.

'That's two of them found, thank God for that,' said Bains.

'We feared the worst,' said Pa. 'We feared the worst for all of you. But thank God, Harry has brought home two of you safely, and if He spares the others they'll be found as well.'

For the first time ever we knew something about the House that the servants didn't know. We gabbled it out in one breath.

'Master George is with the Master,' I said.

'He wasn't on the *Liverpool Lady* when she went down,' said Walter.

'Taken sick in Aden,' said Harry.

There was a moment's dumbfounded silence, and then everybody started talking at once, like a bunch of starlings on a tree.

'There's still the girl unaccounted for,' I heard Joan say. 'That poor child.'

'I went over and whispered, just to her, 'Tweeny is on the *Olympia*, sailing to Australia.'

Her face in the lantern light was a round moon of astonishment and glee. I wish you could have seen her! She took my hand in both hers and squeezed it tight. 'God bless her.'

Harry cycled on ahead to tell Ma that we were quite

safe and very hungry, and Bains rounded up the servants to hurry back to the House and light the fires ready for the gentry. But Pa stayed with us. We walked back home slowly with him, and in that quiet dark we told him the whole story, every detail of it, and he listened to it in silence. When we got to the servants' gate we lingered. We could hear a cab on the drive. That would be the Master and Miss Victoria and Master George. Pa should be at the House to welcome them. But he didn't stride away across the lawns as he could have done, to be at the main door by the time the cab stopped. He stayed with us until he was quite sure that he had heard everything we had to tell him.

'And what have you learned from this?' he asked us at last.

'Not to do anything without telling you first,' Walter said quickly.

'Dorothy?'

I turned away. I couldn't express what was going through my mind, not then. But perhaps Pa knew it already. He bent down and kissed the top of my head, and went off towards the Big House. I still find it hard to put my finger on it, but that was the day I started to grow up.

The Trees Stopped Singing

*I*t wasn't the end of the story.

In the midst of all the fuss and astonishment about the Big House events, we were told at church that England was at war. There was a great 'ah!' of distress among the grown-ups, and the walk home was full of angry, passionate talk. But we could hardly understand all this. War was far away in France and Germany, and here the poppies were bright in the yellow cornfields and the skylark was up there, pouring out its song as if there could never be an end of singing. What was the war to do with us?

But when we got home, Harry stood awkward and proud in the room and told Ma that he was going to be a soldier, and that he was proud to fight for our country. And Ma stood watching him with her hand to her mouth, saying nothing, saying nothing at all, and her silence was like a great tearing cry of grief.

We were all called to a meeting at the Big House about a month later. Not in the servants' hall, but in the drawing room. Master George was there, standing in front of the blue-tiled fireplace with his hands behind his back, next to the Master. Miss Victoria sat by the window, looking out at her beloved conservatory. Miss Caroline, who is now Mrs Eustace Sudley, sat on the chaise longue next to her husband, the Squirrel. They kept sliding their fingers together towards each other. The Dowager was in her Bath chair, beaming at everyone as if it was the Christmas party. She had a jumble of little dolls on her lap, some dressed like servants and some dressed like gentry.

The servants lined the walls. They all looked anxious. Pa was the only one who had his family with him, and we were in our Sunday best. But Harry was not with us. He had gone already, and Ma hadn't smiled or laughed since the day he left.

The Master was his usual cheerful self, although Ma said later that he must be broken in pieces with everything that had happened to him. He spoke very quickly and said a lot that we didn't understand, and I know Joan and Timothy didn't understand much either, the way they kept glancing at each other and puckering up their faces; but it was all to do with the family fortune being reduced.

'And I am having to sell the House,' he finished up.

You could hear the gasp that went round us all. You could feel the room growing cold.

'Master George and I will be returning to Australia, where I will be intending to set up home soon after my marriage to Miss Greenaway. She would not consent to our betrothal until I had brought my son to her; how right she was.'

Master George bowed his head. His eyes were closed tight.

'Miss Victoria and my mother will be moving to a much smaller house in Cheshire, and I am sad to say that we can only retain a handful of staff.'

He stopped, allowing that to sink in. The servants stood rigid. 'Victoria has asked if we can take Miss Bains, of course, and Joan. She will employ a couple of local girls to help them. Lawrence will continue to be chauffeur. The Estate must go, so she can keep no groundsmen, no stablemen, no gardeners, no stables. But, of course, it goes without saying, she will retain Hollins.'

I could feel Pa stiffen beside me.

The Master thanked everyone for their services and their loyalty, and we all filed out. We were all deeply stunned. The Big House was going to be sold!

And it all happened so quickly that we hardly had time to think about it. By the end of the month the gentry had moved and Pa with them. Master George came to our cottage to say goodbye to us, and already he seemed another person. But we had changed too, and those days for running across the fields together and shinning up the sailing ship tree had gone. We didn't have a taste for it any longer. We didn't even think about it.

'I expect we'll keep in touch,' Walter said. But he didn't understand these things. How could we keep in touch?

'I will be going away to school now,' Master George said. 'I'll quite enjoy it, I think, now that I can come home to Father every holiday. And it will be in Australia.'

We had left school that summer, because we were now thirteen. We would get jobs in the city; not as servants, oh no. We were both going to do a typing course and become office workers. We were pleased about it. But our worlds were spinning away from each other, Walter's and mine, ours and Master George's. So Master George said goodbye to us for the second time, and joined his father in the car that was to take them away from the Big House for ever, and I never saw him again.

Until a house was found for us in Cheshire we stayed on in the lodge cottage. We saw Pa whenever he had a day off. It wasn't often, but one Sunday after church we went with Ma and had tea with him in his new pantry. He told us then that his services would not be required after the end of the year. Only Joan and Bains would be kept on, to look after the Dowager.

'Miss Victoria is training to be a nurse,' Pa said, as if there was nothing at all to be surprised at about this statement. And he didn't say this just to Ma. It was for us to hear as well. 'She'll be working with wounded soldiers.'

'She's a different person,' Joan confirmed. 'This war has brought her out of her trance.'

It was a strange thing to say, but I remembered what Tweeny had told us about the letter that Miss Victoria knew off by heart. I told Ma about it on the way home.

'She was once betrothed to a soldier,' Ma said, frowning. 'And he never came back from the Boer War. They said she would never get over it.'

We were the last to leave the estate. The Big House had been bought by the Army as a training school for officers. We saw the great courtyard filling up with strange noisy vehicles. We heard men's voices barking orders in the early morning air. And we saw the end of the trees.

We were having tea one night and telling Ma what we had heard about the war in town. We were suddenly aware of the sound of chopping wood, great thuds that made the cottage shake. Even before we ran to the window we knew what was happening.

'They're chopping the trees down!' shouted Walter.

'What does the army want with trees?' said Ma, and her voice was so grim and bitter that I hardly knew it. One by one, as we watched, the great trees of the drive came crashing down. Walter ran out with a sudden wail and I knew instantly what he was thinking about. I ran after him, and even though the men shouted at us to stand back we ran together to the great chestnut tree, our sailing ship tree. It was lying on the ground, wrenched like a sore tooth out of the soil. I wanted to put my arms round it and lay my face against its warm trunk. It was dead; our tree was dead. We scrabbled among the branches and at last we found what we were looking for – Walter's little black leather story book, *The Adventures of Young Will Tanner*. He clutched it to him, and, that night, in our room, he handed it to me.

'Yours now, Daw.'

From our window we could see clearly the big white house. It looked naked without its fringe of trees; and without the soft drapes of its curtains the windows looked like huge blank eyes, staring at nothing. All around it the trees lay like fallen soldiers.

That was the night that the trees stopped singing.

Walter

Last Word

I suppose you wondered when I was going to have a say! Ah well, I always did find it easier to let Dorothy do the talking for me, even after my stammer had gone.

I found this book you've just been reading some time ago, when Dorothy died. Yes, she went first, poor Daw. I'm the oldest person I know now! I'm a nonagenarian, and that takes a bit of saying even without a stammer. I'd like to live to be a hundred, just to say I've done it. Who knows?

She'd kept her book secret in a little box, along with my black book of stories, *The Adventures of Young Will Tanner*. Took some reading, they did. Crikey! Did I write that? Brought back some memories. And I thought, I won't add to them, I'll leave them just as they are, for the great-grandchildren to read.

I'll tell you something though. This'll please you. This is going back about ten years, when I was just a lad of eighty-three. I took a trip to Liverpool with my daughters – just had a whim to look at the Big House again. Wanted to show them, you see. It belongs to the university now. Nice to think of students living there. I like young people. Haven't got much time for old folk.

Oh, the changes round here! You could run across the fields to Mossley Hill Church at one time, but not any more. All built up. Roads snarled up with cars. Pity. Pity. Still, people have to live, times have to change, don't they?

I stood at the gates, but I didn't know where I was. Our red sandstone cottage had gone. There were a few trees, but they weren't like the old ones, not by a long chalk. Came back to me though. Ghosts. And when I was standing there, I was ten years old again, with my cap in my hand ready to chuck at squirrels.

There was an old man there having a look as well. Now, I know I'm an old man, but I don't think of myself as old, you see. He was a big man, this chap, but stooping a little. He had a young woman with him, helping him to walk down the drive. Couldn't help noticing her, such a mop of wild black hair she had. Australians, both of them.

I turned to my daughters and I said, 'This is where our sailing ship tree was. Should have seen me shinning up there!'

And the old bloke turned round and he looked me up and down as if I was something out of the *Antiques Roadshow*, and then he said, 'It's Walter, isn't it?'

Well, you'll have guessed who he was before I did, I should think. I couldn't get my head round this one. Don't know any Australians – and then it twigged.

'Master George!' I said. 'Crikey! After all these years!'

The college secretary showed us round the house together – painful for me, arthritis, but he wasn't much quicker on his pins. Oh, it's all changed. A ghost house. A haunted house. Can't recognize any of it. We even looked down the cellar. And the woman told us a story about a rocking horse that used to rock on its own. We said nothing.

'What happened to your family, Walter?' he asked me, when we were sitting on a bench in the hall and trying to picture where the stairs used to be.

'Harry came back from the Great War,' I said. 'And fell in love five minutes later. Pa and Ma died just before the Second World War.'

'Dorothy?'

'Oh, she never married,' I said. 'I think she lost her heart to a childhood sweetheart. I miss her. Still miss her. Half of me, you see. Half of me gone.'

He patted my hand. I cry easily these days. I'm not ashamed of it. It just chokes up. Doesn't last. I had to blink a bit though, had to rummage round for something different to talk about.

'Remember that flippin' newt!' And we both chuckled.

'And the good ship *Polly-o*!'

A cleaner pushed a trolley of gadgets and sprays across the hall in front of us, and cast us a wide-eyed, flirty sort of look, big smile on her face. 'All right, boys?' she said.

'Wonder what happened to Tweeny?' I said. 'I don't suppose anyone ever heard of her again.'

'Ah, Tweeny!' Master George laughed. 'Matter of fact, I did. She landed at Melbourne and somehow got herself ashore without papers and went straight to Miss Greenaway. Offered her services in exchange for being taught to read and write. And the lady was rather taken with her, you know. Tweeny had a bit of spirit, and that's what Australians like. Tell you something about Australians, Walter. There's none of this Master George business out there. They're all equal. I soon learnt that when I went out to live there.'

'She looked a fine sight in my togs,' I chuckled. 'I hope she did well for herself.'

'I think she did all right.' Master George stood up, stretching his back with a contented sigh, like an old cat, and his granddaughter came over to help him. 'She married me,' he said, 'and this is our grandchild, Mary.'

And that's it. Now you know everything. Tweeny and Dorothy have both gone, the tree has gone. Pity. Pity. But the Big House in Liverpool that drew us all together is still there, full of young people looking to their own bright future. I wish them happy lives.

Also by Berlie Doherty published by Catnip

Children of Winter

Out walking, deep in the Derbyshire hills, Catherine and her family are forced to take shelter from a sudden storm in an old barn.

It all seems strangely familiar to Catherine. As the torchlight dims, shadows of the past crowd in, memories of a time hundreds of years ago, when three children took refuge in a barn, not from a storm but from a terrible plague…

This gripping and haunting adventure is inspired by the true story of the village of Eyam which in 1665 cut itself off from the rest of Derbyshire, so that no other village would catch the Plague.

"Vividly and sensitively realised"
Guardian

Granny was a Buffer Girl

'You tell your secrets and I'll tell mine,' said Granny Dorothy. 'I'll tell you something that Albert doesn't know, even. My best secret.'

Mum did catch my eye then, and her look promised me that I wouldn't be going away from home without sharing all its secrets, and all its love stories, and all its ghost stories too.

Jess is 18 and leaving home for the first time. Her family get together to celebrate and share the stories of their lives – stories of love and adventure, of happiness and loss, of promises and secrets.

"A compelling and unusual book"
Times Educational Supplement

"Vividly evocative of time and place, a poignant portrait of a dozen individuals whose joys and trials are universal"
Kirkus

Winner of the Carnegie Medal

Praise for Berlie Doherty

"Berlie Doherty captures the magic of human emotion"
Grace Kempster, Books For Keeps

"Berlie Doherty writes both for adults and children,
moving easily across the divide"
Guardian

"What a marvellous writer… one who uses language as if
it has been newly invented"
Junior Bookshelf